MW00616045

ALSO BY JENELLE LEANNE SCHMIDT

A CLASSIC RETOLD SERIES

Learn more at AClassicRetold.com

ENDORSEMENTS

Jenelle L. Schmidt's "Steal the Morrow," a fantasy retelling of Oliver Twist, is anything but derivative. Set in an immersive, immediately-believable realm, Steal the Morrow will first steal your heart and then catapult you into a harrowing tale that somehow leaves you both breathless and hopeful. A must read for Fantasy and Dickens fans alike.

— WAYNE THOMAS BATSON, *BESTSELLING AUTHOR OF THE DOOR WITHIN TRILOGY AND THE EPIC MYRIDIAN CONSTELLATION*

Steal the Morrow is a delightful reimagining of Dickens' Oliver Twist. The home and family the orphaned, noble Olifur finds in the forest and then must work hard to return to are every adventurous child's dream! Highly recommended.

— E.J. KITCHENS, *AUTHOR OF THE MAGIC COLLECTORS STORIES*

Jenelle L. Schmidt crafted a fun adventure story full of friendship and life lessons for the whole family. Olifur is an endearing young boy who brings out the child-like heart and awe in all of us.

— RALENE BURKE, *AUTHOR OF THE SACRED ARMOR TRILOGY*

Charles Dickens meets Middle Earth ... Steal the Morrow takes the gritty realism of Charles Dickens' England and transports it to a world highlighted by fantastical creatures and unique technology. The world building has the depth of a Tolkien book, without overpowering the heart wrenching story ... The struggles in the great outdoors and in the heart of the city provide an inspiring take of overcoming adversity with integrity.

— ALLEN BROKKEN, *AUTHOR OF THE TOWERS OF LIGHT SERIES*

Steal the Morrow gives Charles Dickens a run for his money! The hero, Olifur, will steal your heart. Full of wistful beauty and enthralling characters, Steal the Morrow is at once hopeful and heartbreaking. A study in the contrast of light and dark of our world, the story sweeps you from the beauty of grace, kindness, and sharing into the heart of darkness where thievery and cruelty rule the day.

— S.L. DOOLEY, *AUTHOR OF THE PORTAL SLAYER TRILOGY*

A CLASSIC RETOLD

STEAL THE MORROW

JENELLE LEANNE SCHMIDT

Steal the Morrow

Part of the A Classic Retold series

By Jenelle Leanne Schmidt

Copyright 2023 by Jenelle Leanne Schmidt

Published by Stormcave

www.jenelleschmidt.com

Steal the Morrow

ISBN: 978-1-960357-98-4

This is a work of fiction. All of the characters, organizations, and events portrayed in
this novel are either products of the author's rather large and vivid imagination, or
are used fictitiously. Any resemblance to persons real or historical is purely
coincidental.

Cover art by Miblart

Book design by Declan Rowe

CONTENTS

For Brittany: you are golden.

"It is because I think so much of warm and sensitive hearts, that I would spare them from being wounded."

— CHARLES DICKENS; *OLIVER TWIST*

1

BANDITS!

The carriage rumbled along the road, bouncing lightly. Olifur sat next to his mother, gripping her hand. In his other arm, he held a stuffed animal that had once resembled an elephant, but after seven years of being loved fiercely by a little boy now looked like nothing so much as a lumpy, gray potato. He whimpered slightly, his eyes fixed on his mother's pale face. She looked so frail, nothing like his energetic, strong mother. The shadows of the trees they were passing swept across her face like a ghostly caress. The shadows terrified him, and he flinched at the way they illuminated the gauntness of her cheeks and the dullness in her eyes. What if she didn't get better? What if the physicians couldn't do any more than their village healer had?

She squeezed his fingers gently. "Don't worry, Olifur," she whispered. "Your father will get us to the sychstal in Melar. The physician there will help me. It's not far, now."

He nodded, but her reassuring words could not ease the dread coiling like a serpent in his belly. The wagon hit another bump and his mother moaned.

Olifur burrowed into her side with another whimper. She kissed his head.

"The Builder will care for us," she whispered. "We must always trust him."

"Please, Builder," Olifur thought, "please let the physician be able to heal her." He wondered if the Builder could hear him. Mama and Papa had often told him that the Builder was not the distant, uncaring being that many thought him to be, but Olifur wasn't sure. If the Builder really cared, then why had he allowed Mama to get so sick?

"Hold the coach!"

Olifur's eyes flew to the window of their carriage at the sound of the rough voice. He could not see out, not while sitting. His mother's fingers tightened painfully on his, preventing him from rising to peer out the window. The serpent within him tightened its coils as the carriage slowed. Were they being stopped by soldiers? Papa had said that the roads were much safer since the Ar'Mol had conquered the other warlords and brought peace and stability to the realm the year Olifur was born, but there were still pockets of resistance.

"Please, my wife is very ill. It is urgent that I get her to the sychstal." Papa's voice drifted back to them. "We don't have any coin."

"What was you planning on paying the healers wif, then?" the rough voice growled.

Papa's voice thinned and lowered, too soft for Olifur's ears to catch, though some of the words carried to him. "Every last coin... nothing has worked... our last chance... please..." The carriage jerked as though someone had bumped it forcefully. His mother gave a shuddering moan.

"Then we'll just have to take your fine leythan and carriage. We keep these roads safe, but only for paying customers," another voice jeered.

"But my wife..."

"Ain't no concern of ours, now is she?"

The door to the carriage burst open and a large face peered in. "Come on out of there."

Olifur squeezed his mother's hand so tightly his fingers grew stiff. He glowered at the man. "Leave my mother alone! She's sick!" he shouted.

The man guffawed. "This little un's got spirit, Bale! And the sick woman's in here, like 'e said."

"Get them both out," a deeper voice called back.

The man reached in, his long arm gripping Olifur's mother's ankles as if to slide her straight out of the carriage. Provoked to righteous fury, Olifur sprang at the man with a shout, his small fist swinging at the man's rough face.

He never landed the blow. The man's massive paw snatched him up by the front of his shirt and Olifur hung from his grasp, snarling and kicking helplessly.

"The lad thinks he's a grymstalker cub!" the man shouted, a cruel grin spreading across his face.

"Put me down!" Olifur shouted.

"Gladly." The man opened his hand and Olifur dropped heavily to the hard-packed earth. Landing on his back, Olifur's breath exploded out of him painfully, leaving him gasping on the ground. Dismissing the boy, the bandit returned his attention to the woman, yanking her out of the carriage and depositing her in the dust. She let out a weak cry.

At this, Olifur struggled to his feet and attacked the man's leg with the only weapon he had.

The man shrieked and kicked, prying him away from his leg and shoving him so that he stumbled back and sat on the ground, hard.

"Little cubling bit me!" the man growled.

The leader, the one called Bale, chortled. "Never turn your back on a grymstalker, Cuyler, no matter how small it is."

Cuyler aimed a kick his way, which Olifur only partially dodged. The man's boot connected with his side, knocking him over. Olifur sniffled as tears sprang to his eyes. He scrambled over to his mother, pressing himself against her side. Where was Papa?

"Mama!"

She awkwardly wrapped an arm around him, pulling him close. "We will be all right, Oli. The Builder will care for us. Always follow the Builder, my son. No matter what happens." There was a desperate urgency in her voice that frightened Olifur almost as much as the men looming over them.

"Let us go!" Papa's voice rang out, and terror gripped Olifur as he saw the tall, dark-haired leader coming to the back of the carriage, shoving Papa ahead of him. He held Papa's arm wrenched behind his back at an odd angle.

"We are letting you go," Bale snarled, shoving Papa toward his wife and son.

Papa stumbled forward, then gained his balance and whirled. "You cannot do this," he said, his voice low and pleading. "Please. The boy needs his mother. Please let us go on our way. We just need to get to Melar; we're so close. Leaving us here is the same as killing her."

The bandits merely cackled. Papa's face grew grim and stern, and Olifur huddled against his mother at the sudden fury he saw in his father's expression. A glint of something in Papa's hand caught the sunlight as he dove at the leader.

Olifur barely had time to blink. Everything happened so fast. The bandit leader whirled. A hiss split the air. Papa fell limply to the ground without a sound. The dirt near his face turned red.

Mama leaped to her feet with a wordless scream and dashed toward Papa with a strength Olifur hadn't seen in her in a long time. Her voice rose into a wail and she screamed Papa's name over and over. Olifur stared, not sure what had happened. Why did Papa just lie there? Why didn't he get up?

Mama hurled something at the bandit leader, something sharp and terrible, that lodged itself in his thin shoulder. With a hiss of pain, the man snarled and spun. He clutched at the knife in his shoulder, pulling it out with a growl. Blood dripped down his shoulder and the blade shone red. The bandit glared at it for a moment, then he struck, his hand moving faster than Olifur could track with his eyes. Mama's screaming stopped with a deafening suddenness, and she fell forward onto the ground next to Papa.

Olifur stared at his parents. Silently, he urged them to rise. To get up. What had happened to his strong, laughing father? Why did he let these men take their carriage? Why did he lie there on the ground? Why did Mama stare up at the sky, unmoving?

A strange sound filled his ears, and it took him a moment to realize it was his own voice, rising in a wailing scream.

The bandits turned to stare at him, and Olifur froze, clamping his mouth shut. Fear spiked through him and he felt himself tremble. He wrapped his arms around his beloved elephant and squeezed his eyes shut, waiting for the pain he knew would come. The one called Bale loomed over him, his dark eyes burning into Olifur's memory, his narrow face set in an expression of murderous rage that Olifur knew he would carry with him until the day he died.

"What should we do about the cub?" Cuyler asked.

"Nothing," Bale grunted, turning his back on the boy.

"Just leave him out here?" Cuyler asked.

"World don't need another orphan hanging around," Bale muttered. "Let the wilderness be the end of him."

Without another word, the two men climbed up into the saddles attached to the backs of their huge leythan. The beasts rumbled forward on well-muscled legs. Cuyler shot Olifur an ugly grin as he grabbed the reins of Papa's carriage leythan. The gentle beast bellowed mournfully, its scaled sides heaving, but it did not protest as the man began leading the beast and the carriage away.

"Bet the grymstalkers find you tonight," Cuyler called out with a harsh laugh. "Try biting one of *them*."

They kicked their own leythan into a trot and soon they and the carriage disappeared over the next rise, leaving Olifur alone on the road.

Tears leaked down Olifur's face as he squeezed his elephant

tighter. Mama and Papa still lay unmoving in the dirt, the ground around them turning crimson. As the sound of the lumbering leythan faded away, the fear coiling inside him released enough for him to approach his fallen parents.

"M-Mama?" he whispered through trembling lips. "P-Papa? They're gone. You can get up now."

2

A GRIEVOUS BUSINESS

They were dead. Olifur understood this in a distant way that didn't seem real. He understood death. He had once had a pet bird that had died. He had found it lying at the bottom of its cage, and it had taken him a long time to understand that the creature would never wake up again. But this was so much more painful than that had been. This throbbing ache in his heart that clawed its way up his throat and burned in his eyes could surely never be comforted or diminished. He knelt in the dust and sobbed.

For hours he knelt there, unaware of anything around him. Unconscious of the sun slipping away. Heedless of anything other than the fact that his world had just ended and he had nothing. When he had exhausted his entire store of tears, Olifur sat frozen and numb, staring at the bodies that used to be his parents. His entire being felt hollow, drained.

As the sky above him darkened, the air cooled, and he shivered. Olifur finally rose to his feet and looked around. Night was drawing near. The trees of the small wood they had been traveling through loomed above him like ominous giants on one side of the road, and a jagged cliff rose on the other. A good place for an ambush. Numbly, he looked at his parents. They should be buried. As young as he was, he knew this, in a sort of distant way. He remembered his father helping him bury the bird. But he had no shovel. No way to properly put them to rest. He sniffled as tears sprang back to his dry eyes. Large boulders lay scattered at the base of the cliff. Perhaps he could set them over his parents' bodies?

Slowly, Olifur made his way over to the base of the cliff and tried to pick up a boulder. His arms strained, but he could not lift it. Dejectedly, he sat down, his eyes burning once more. After another few minutes, Olifur rose and chose a smaller rock. Struggling to lift it, he carried it to the road and laid it next to his mother. Then he slowly returned to the cliff for another stone.

It took him all night.

Back and forth. Back and forth. Step after step. Stone after stone. The weight of them piled up on his shoulders, bowing them, even as he stacked the rocks in a crude monument. Sweat beaded on his face, pouring into his eyes, dripping from his short hair. His breaths came in labored gasps, and his legs and arms felt as feeble as grass by the time a thin line of gold started to illuminate the clouds above him. Olifur placed the final stone and fell to the ground in an exhausted stupor.

The world around him moved. The sun rose, the wind blew, birds sang, but Olifur was unconscious of it all. His body ached and his soul wailed, a long, continuous, unceasing lament that he no longer had any tears to express. He closed his eyes and slept.

When he awoke, dark clouds had rolled across the sky, threatening a storm. He had no idea how long he had slept. He felt as heavy and stiff as the stones he had moved. Olifur hugged his elephant and huddled closer to his parents' cairn. Hunger gnawed at his belly. He had never really been hungry before, not like this, and now the anguish of genuine hunger and thirst made him curl up into a ball. He longed for a sip of water, but did not know where to find any.

A twig nearby cracked, and Olifur's heart raced. The bandit's parting comment about grymstalkers drifted through his thoughts and he leaped up and dashed to the base of the cliff where he ducked behind the nearest boulder, clutching his elephant to his chest and silently begging the Builder to care about him for just a moment.

He peeked out over a boulder and then ducked back down with a terrified gasp. Green eyes gleamed in the trees, growing steadily larger.

"Builder, please," the child whimpered, unable to keep the sound from escaping his lips.

The enormous cat emerged from the forest. Its huge paws padded softly, barely making a sound as it stalked closer. Its eyes blazed like green fire, and its mouth hung open, revealing sharp teeth. Muscles rippled beneath silky gray fur.

Fear quaked through him as Olifur peeked through the rocks, heart thumping as though it might burst from his chest. But the massive beast did not seem to notice him.

A tall man swung down from the cat's back, and Olifur's eyes widened in surprise. What sort of man could tame and ride a grymstalker?

"What have we here?" the man muttered.

He strode up to the pile of rocks, tilting his head this way and that as he circled the crude cairn. He knelt down near the edge of the construction, stretching a hand out as if to pick up one of the stones.

Olifur burst out from behind his boulder. "Don't you touch them!" he screamed, anger overwhelming his fear, though he kept himself as far as he could from the creature. "Leave them alone!"

The man reared back, his eyes widening at the sight of the small boy. "I don't mean any harm, lad." His voice was rough but kind. He stared thoughtfully at the child for a long moment, then he dropped his gaze to the stones, his eyes flicking back and forth between the small boy and the rough cairn. After a long moment, he spoke again. "These your parents?"

Olifur glared at the man. "Yes. You leave them alone!"

The man glanced up and down the road, but stayed kneeling,

inspecting the construction of the tomb. Olifur studied the man warily. A tattered cloak hung from broad shoulders. He had large, muscular arms that were banded with leather straps. Leather bracers adorned both his wrists. Wild black hair and a bushy dark beard, both streaked with a generous helping of gray, adorned the man's head and face. Dark blue eyes peered out from a weather-beaten and sun-darkened face. At least he wasn't a grymstalker. But was this man another bandit? He carried a long bow, with a quiver of arrows slung over his back, and Olifur glimpsed a hatchet and a dagger hanging from his belt. The boy shuddered at the sight of the weapons, remembering the flash of sunlight on steel and pools of crimson.

The man's gaze now moved to Olifur. "You build this?" He gestured at the cairn.

Olifur nodded, tears trickling down his face once more. He was too tired to be afraid of the man, too hungry and heartsore to feel much of anything.

"Were you heading to Melar?"

Olifur gulped. "Yes, sir."

"Family there?"

Olifur shook his head. "Healers for my mama..." The tears returned in earnest. "Bandits attacked us."

The man stood, stretched, and stared up at the cloudy sky. The breeze picked up, and they could hear a distant rumble of thunder. Olifur shivered and gave a low whimper.

The man scowled down at him. "Stop your cryin' and come along with me if you've a mind to." He stomped away, not following the road, but plunging back into the woods. The grym-stalker paced beside him, its tail flicking back and forth.

Olifur hesitated for a moment, uncertain. The man might be a villain. But he had made no threatening movements. Despite his rough appearance and gruff words, he had somehow seemed kind. And he was an adult who might have access to food and water. Olifur waffled, loath to leave this spot—the last tie to his home and parents. And yet he could not survive here, alone.

Another rumble of thunder, this one louder and closer, decided him. Olifur, squeezing his stuffed animal tightly with one arm, darted into the trees after the man.

Olifur had to jog to catch up, but he warily stayed behind the man, who did not slow his pace. They did not follow any kind of noticeable trail, and Olifur found it difficult to keep up. He kept stumbling over roots and getting tangled up in vines. The man tromped ahead, never looking back to make sure Olifur could keep up, never offering a word of encouragement or a hand of help, just winding his way through the forest with unwavering confidence. The enormous cat followed sedately, also taking no notice of the small person following their trail.

Olifur struggled to move his weary legs, forcing his body to keep going. If he let the man out of his sight, he would be hopelessly lost. The fear of wandering through the dark forest alone until a wild beast found and ate him was the only thing that kept him moving. The long hours of weary labor, the short sleep, the lack of food or water all combined to drag at his muscles and prick the backs of his eyes. But the man had ordered him to stop crying, so Olifur valiantly held back his tears.

At long last, they reached a clearing, and the man stopped, gesturing grandly. "Home," he barked.

Olifur stared.

In the center of the glade stood a massive fireplace, open on both sides and built of stone. A large fire blazed, the smoke traveling up the large chimney. Worn, patchwork hammocks hung between immense trees that circled the clearing. High in the branches, someone had strung a tattered canopy above the hammocks, a poor protection from the elements. Off to one side stood two structures: a simple log cabin with a thatched roof, and a much smaller, narrower sort of house with walls made of planks and a roof covered in slats of wood with a stovepipe sticking out of it. A smokehouse, Olifur realized, recognizing it as similar to the one his papa had built back home.

"The lads'll make you welcome," the man said. "Lorcan! Come, welcome our new friend."

Without another word, the older man turned and strode back into the forest. Olifur stared after him with wide eyes, wondering what he was supposed to do now.

"What's your name? Your name?"

The friendly, if somewhat strange, words startled Olifur, and he turned to look up into the hazel eyes of an older boy.

"Olifur." He squeezed his stuffed animal tightly.

"Hey, Olifur. I'm Lorcan. Welcome to Fritjof's Glen. Fritjof's Glen. First thing to do. Must do the first things first. We better find you a hammock. Come along." The older boy trotted away toward the trees and Olifur followed him slowly, his head spinning.

They reached the trees, and Lorcan eyed Olifur dubiously. "You're pretty small. Hoy, Kellen! Give me a hand, here. First thing first. We need to lower one of the empty hammocks for Olifur here. Olifur is our new friend."

A dark, curly head popped up from a hammock quite a ways off the ground and brown eyes peered down at Olifur. "A new friend? Where'd Fritjof find him?"

Lorcan shrugged. "You know Fritjof. Not much for talking. Not much at all. Come on down and you can ask him yourself."

The boy, nearly as small as Olifur himself, swung himself easily out of the hammock and spiraled down a rope that Olifur hadn't even noticed hanging from a branch high above. He landed lightly on the ground and slung an arm around Olifur's shoulders.

"I'm Kellen! What's your story?"

Olifur's eyes stung. "My parents were killed."

Kellen gave a shrug of one shoulder. "Well, of course they were. All of us here are orphans. Even Fritjof."

Olifur sniffled.

"Leave him be, Kellen," Lorcan said gruffly. "Help me move this hammock closer to the ground, won't you? Must be closer to the ground. Don't want young Olifur to fall out and break his neck tonight. No more new friend, then."

Kellen nodded cheerfully and together, the two boys made quick work of lowering the hammock and securing it.

"You can keep any of your own belongings in your hammock," Kellen told Olifur. "Nobody here will touch anything in another boy's hammock."

"That's the second rule. Fritjof says that the Builder frowns on stealing," Lorcan said. "The rules are important. There are rules. Rules are good. I have to go get some more firewood, and the others will be back soon. Kellen, you keep an eye on our new friend."

Kellen nodded amiably as Lorcan left.

"He's... different," Olifur said, watching the older boy go.

"A bit," Kellen agreed amiably. "His brain works too fast, Fritjof says. But he's steady with his work. He's a stickler for the rules, but he's a good sort, even if all his hens aren't home."

Olifur squeezed his elephant, then placed it carefully in the hammock. "How many rules are there?" he asked.

"Just two," Kellen said.

"What's the first rule, then?" Olifur asked.

"If you want to eat, you pull your weight," Kellen replied. "The first night you're a guest. If you want to stay longer, you have to work."

"What kind of work?" Olifur asked, wondering if it involved climbing around in the trees some more. He kind of wished that the two older boys hadn't moved his hammock quite so close to the ground. He liked to climb, and the idea of sleeping up in the trees seemed interesting, and safer from grymstalkers.

"Oh, all kinds." Kellen shrugged. "Hunting, cooking, cleaning up, that sort of thing. Keeping the cabin fixed up, watching the fire. But don't worry, Fritjof will teach you everything you need to know. Just make sure you listen good, because he doesn't talk much, and he never gives instructions twice. You're supposed to pay attention the first time."

Olifur nodded earnestly.

"You tired?" Kellen asked.

Olifur nodded. His entire body still ached from the long night of work, and his feet were sore after the long hike trying to keep up with his new benefactor. His stomach rumbled loudly.

"Hungry, too." Kellen grinned. "Here." He pulled a chunk of dried meat from his pocket and offered it to Olifur. "Fritjof will be back soon with dinner, but this will help for now. You should try out your hammock."

Grateful to the other boy for his generosity, Olifur took the proffered meat and clambered into the hammock, which promptly flipped over and dumped him on the ground. He lay on his back, a little stunned at first. Kellen's grinning face appeared above him.

"They can be a little tricky at first. That's why we all start out close to the ground," the other boy said, holding out a hand to help Olifur back to his feet. "You'll get the hang of it. Try again."

This time, Olifur got himself into the swinging contraption without knocking his breath from his lungs. He lay on his back, the hammock swinging slightly.

"Comfortable?" Kellen asked.

Olifur nodded.

"Good. I'm just up a row if you need something. We usually sleep in the hammocks. The cabin is just for bad weather, but it's pretty cramped with all of us in there. And the weather in this part of Turrim is usually pretty nice. Thought it was going to storm earlier, but it seems to have blown over." Kellen's face disappeared and Olifur munched on the dried meat, staring up at the branches overhead, his elephant clutched in his arm once more. Despite the precarious nature of the hammock, and the lack of walls or a roof, Olifur felt safe for the first time in two days. The bright green of the leaves mesmerized him as he swayed back and forth beneath them. The gentle rocking lulled him into a drowsy contentment, and he slowly let his eyelids flutter closed.

3

FRITJOF'S GLEN

Olifur startled awake and lay blinking up at the branches, wondering where he was. All the events of the previous day crashed over him. Grief gripped him tightly, like a giant claw pressing down on his chest. He gulped through his sobs, trying not to make any noise or draw any attention to himself. Wrapping his arms around himself, Olifur burrowed under his blanket, hiccoughing through tears that seemed like they could never end. A gentle breeze ruffled through his hair like a caress and Olifur quietly cried himself back to sleep.

When he next awoke, it was to a commotion outside his hammock. Its eruption drowned out even his own thoughts. With some effort, he lifted himself to his knees—it was a wobbly business, but he managed it—and peeked over the edge of his new bed. His eyes felt swollen and gritty, and a tight rawness scratched at his throat as he swallowed. Through groggy eyes, he looked out upon the glen. The sun seemed to be settling down behind the trees, and a large fire blazed in the great stone fireplace, casting a warm glow across the little clearing. Fritjof had returned, and with him were about a dozen boys of various sizes. They capered about as he swung a large deer down from his shoulders. Olifur blinked as everyone set to work. Each child, from the largest to the smallest, seemed to have some preassigned role in preparing the meal.

Olifur spotted the familiar curly hair of Kellen and watched as the boy went over to Fritjof and started speaking. They were too far away for Olifur to hear any of the words, but Fritjof appeared to listen intently, nodding as the boy spoke. They both glanced his way, and Olifur ducked down into his hammock, hoping he hadn't been noticed.

A moment later, Kellen's face peeked over the folds of the hammock. "I thought I saw you waking up over here," the boy said cheerfully. "Come on, everyone wants to meet you. Bet you're hungry, eh?"

Olifur tried to press himself deeper into the hammock, shaking his head in sudden shyness, but then his own stomach turned traitorous, rumbling loudly. Kellen reached down and grabbed Olifur's arm, pulling him up and tipping the hammock until it dumped him out.

"There's nothing to be afraid of," Kellen assured him. "It's all a little overwhelming at first, I know, but you'll soon feel at home. Being a guest is the hardest. Once you join the family, you always know what your job is and things. No sitting around feeling awkward anymore. There's always work to be done."

Olifur allowed himself to be pulled closer to the fire, into the throng of boys. Most were older than him. They greeted him with good humor, introducing themselves in a cacophony of names and faces that swam before his eyes. Surely he would never remember which faces went with which names. He gave his own name several times and told his story more than once before Fritjof finally intervened.

"Quit badgering him," the old man barked. He pushed Olifur down onto a log, not unkindly, and waved the long wooden ladle he was using to stir the venison stew that the boys had made. "Get our guest a bowl, lads! Can't you see he's about to fall over from hunger?"

Someone thrust a crude wooden bowl into Olifur's hands,

along with a flattened stick that he guessed was supposed to be a spoon. Fritjof ladled a thick, hearty stew into his bowl, and then the other boys lined up for their own food, becoming an orderly line as if by some unseen magic.

Olifur sat on the log in a daze and stared down at his bowl. The idea of stew perplexed him. His parents had not been wealthy, and though his family had never gone hungry, their fare had been simple. He had been used to porridge and eggs for most meals, or perhaps toast with some of his mother's preserves. Occasionally, she would roast a chicken, but that had been before she had gotten sick... His eyes burned as he thought of his parents. Swiping the back of his hand across his face to hide his sudden tears, Olifur took a large bite of the stew.

The first sip burned Olifur's tongue, but he was so hungry he barely noticed. The pangs of hunger had long since subsided, but at the first taste of food they returned with roaring force. Within seconds, he had gulped down the entire bowlful. The other boys sat around on logs, eating at a more sedate pace and talking and joking with one another. Olifur stared at the stewpot longingly. His stomach clenched, still ravenously hungry. Fritjof sat silently apart from the boys, his eyes drifting about the clearing with a sort of watchful alertness, his own bowl held loosely as he spooned stew into his own mouth.

Gathering up all the courage he had ever possessed, Olifur forced himself to stand. Slowly, he crossed the short distance that felt like miles and stood before the man who had rescued him. Fritjof cocked his head to one side, staring down at him expectantly. Olifur opened his mouth, but no sound came out.

"Well?" Fritjof prompted after a long silence.

Olifur licked his lips and gave a small croak. "Please, sir." His voice came out in a thin, wavering stream. "May I have some more?"

Fritjof's face broke into a wide, beaming smile. "Like our stew, do you?"

Olifur nodded.

The man snatched Olifur's bowl from his hands and ushered him to the fire. He ladled several hearty spoonfuls into the bowl and handed it back. "By all means, have as much as you like."

"Th-thank you," Olifur said.

"Welcome," Fritjof grunted. He eyed Olifur. "Melar is only about fifteen miles north of here. You said you don't have any family there?"

Olifur shook his head. He savored the warmth of the stew.

"Where are you from?"

Olifur squinted. "Mjolvar."

"That far?" Fritjof's eyebrows rose. "That's a long way to travel."

"Mama was sick," Olifur explained. "The healers near us couldn't do anything for her. But they said there was a physician in Melar who could help."

"You have any family back in Mjolvar? Friends you might want to stay with?"

Olifur shook his head again. "No, sir."

"Hmm." Fritjof stared at him. "Well, you can stay with us if you like. Or I can take you into Melar and try to find you an apprenticeship if you'd rather."

A wave of panic washed through Olifur at the thought of leaving. Fritjof seemed gruff and hard, but he had also been kind. "I'd like to stay, please," he stammered.

Fritjof eyed him. "You sure? Our life here is not easy. I don't tolerate laziness."

Olifur's thoughts wandered to the things Kellen and Lorcan had said earlier. "I'll help wash up."

Fritjof chuckled. "That's a good lad. But no, you rest tonight, and watch. Tomorrow we'll put you to work, find you a place in our school."

"School?" Olifur asked.

"As such." The man shrugged one shoulder.

"Are you a teacher?" Olifur liked school. He had only been old enough to attend one year, and his attendance had not been steady, what with his mother's illness. But he had enjoyed learning his letters and numbers. He wondered if this strange man in the wilderness would teach him now.

"Of a kind," Fritjof replied. "Oh, not numbers and letters. But you'll learn how to survive out here. Which plants are good for eating. Which are poisonous. Which ones will heal. Tomorrow, you'll start making your first bow, and you'll learn to shoot it so that you can help with the hunting."

Olifur stared at the man. "All that?"

"All that and more." Kellen came up and punched Olifur lightly in the shoulder. "How to start a fire, how to tan a hide, how to sew your own clothes, and all sorts of other things you need to know how to do to survive out here."

"But for tonight, you rest," Fritjof reiterated. "Eat your stew."

Olifur nodded numbly. He stumbled a little as he returned to his spot. The stew in his bowl had cooled, but he ate it more slowly anyway, savoring the bites of meat and the chunks of vegetables: wild onions and mushrooms and a few greens he couldn't identify. Kellen sat with him, telling a story about something, but Olifur wasn't listening. He was too busy looking around the camp with new eyes.

"Kellen," he interrupted his new friend. "Is everyone here really an orphan?"

"Yeah," Kellen replied, pausing mid-sentence. "Didn't I say that earlier?"

"Where'd they all come from?"

"Oh, here and there." Kellen shrugged. "Fritjof seems to have a knack for finding us when we need him."

"I'm glad he found me." Olifur's nose prickled, and he rubbed it, trying to hold back the tears that threatened to spill down into his stew.

"It doesn't stop hurting," Kellen said, as though aware of Olifur's thoughts. "But it gets easier to bear. And Fritjof keeps us busy. Having work to do helps."

Olifur took another bite of stew and chewed, swallowing it

down past the lump in his throat. "And he'll really teach me all those things? Making a fire, hunting? Things like that?"

"Aye." Kellen grinned.

"Why?" Olifur asked, wondering why the old man would care about a bunch of orphans.

Kellen gave a shrug. "We've asked him that a couple of times. But all he'll ever say about it is that someone once did the same for him."

"I wonder who it was?"

"I think he means the Builder," Kellen said. "But I'm not sure. He's never real clear about it. Fritjof doesn't talk much. Your conversation with him tonight was the most words I think I've ever heard him say all at once."

Olifur nodded, accepting the information. Another thought struck him. "Kellen? Are there any wild grymstalkers in these woods?"

Kellen squinted one eye. "I've never seen one. But I've heard one scream once. It really does sound like screaming. Not hissing or caterwauling or nothing like that. It's a sound'll freeze the blood in your veins."

Olifur shivered. "Don't you worry? Sleeping outside like this?"

Kellen shook his head. "Nah. Fritjof protects us. And Bet."

"Who's Bet?" Olifur asked.

"Fritjof's malkyn," Kellen said. "You saw her."

"Oh." Olifur nodded, shivering as he remembered the terror that had overwhelmed him before he realized the enormous cat was tame. "I thought she was a grymstalker," he confessed, feeling slightly ashamed of his fear.

Kellen gave a chuckle. "She'll fight like one to protect us," he said. "But she's no grymstalker. Those beasts have enormous teeth that curl down over their lower jaw. Haven't you ever seen a malkyn before?"

"Once," Olifur said, the memory coming faintly back to him

of a time a year ago when he and his parents had made a rare trip into town. "It was a long time ago."

"Besides, grymstalkers don't like fires, and they don't like people. And we've got both here in the glen. Don't worry. You're safe as a fox in its den here," Kellen reassured him.

Olifur felt himself relax a bit at Kellen's comforting words. He scraped the last bite of stew out of his bowl and gulped it down.

Kellen grinned at him. "More?" he teased.

Olifur shook his head. "No. I'm so full, I might burst!"

Later, there were stories around the fire as the stars began to appear, speckling the blackness of the sky. The clouds had long since blown away, leaving the view overhead clear. The logs on the fire popped, sending sparks up into the air. Olifur listened to the others talk, feeling full and comfortable and drowsy. He felt his head bobbing slightly, and then he was being gathered up in powerful arms. Fritjof carried him across the clearing and deposited him into his hammock. Olifur felt a rough blanket pulled up over him and tucked beneath his chin. He heard Fritjof's voice as the man stumped back to the fire, telling the other boys it was time for bed. And then he lay there, drifting away from the waking hours, listening to the popping crackle of the fire, the gentle buzzing of night bugs, and the faint hooting of an owl somewhere over the forest. And then all was darkness and peace as sleep finally claimed him.

4

FRITJOF'S SCHOOL

Olifur woke to Kellen shaking him in the still-dark of early morning. He blinked up at the older boy and yawned.

"We rise early here," Kellen said. "Lots to do."

Olifur blinked the sleep out of his eyes and nodded groggily. He slumped out of his hammock and stood, yawning and rubbing his face.

"You'll start out by helping with the fire," Kellen explained. "It's a simple job, but it takes concentration. Everyone starts there."

Olifur nodded, trying to hide his disappointment. He had fallen asleep dreaming of learning to use a longbow and of going hunting with Fritjof, tramping through the woods and learning all its wonders and secrets. Tending the fire lacked the same appeal. But he did not want to seem ungrateful, so he trotted after Kellen over to the smoking coals. The large hearth was still warm, but the fire inside had died down to embers.

Kellen took Olifur into the trees and showed him how to find dry sticks for tinder. Then they hiked back to the stone chimney, and Kellen taught him how to coax the embers back into flames.

"Tomorrow, you'll do this by yourself," he explained. "If the coals have gone out before you get up, you can use the flint and steel to make sparks. Here, I'll show you how."

Kellen demonstrated, then told Olifur to make his own little tinder pile and try his hand at starting a fire. It took him a dozen tries, but he finally got the sparks to light the tinder, and he soon had a merry little fire blazing on one side of the hearth. Kellen showed him how to feed the fire without getting too close, and Olifur watched carefully, committing every movement to memory. At last, Kellen gave an approving nod.

"I think you've got it," he said. "Today, you watch the fire and make certain it doesn't go out. It's important. Without the fire, we can't make our meals."

Olifur nodded, though his heart sank a little. All day watching the fire? He glanced longingly at the fishing poles and longbows hanging from pegs along a thick branch off to one side of the glen and heaved a sigh.

Kellen, following his glance, gave him a grin and ruffled his hair. "Soon enough," he promised. "Everyone learns how to hunt and fish, too. But you have to earn the privilege. Do a good job with the fire and your other chores as they come along, and before you know it, Fritjof will take you along on one of his rambles."

With this promise hanging in the air, Kellen left Olifur to tend the fire, and disappeared.

He had too much time to think as he sat and watched the fire. Visions of the bandits kept crowding into his thoughts every time he blinked. The terror he had experienced at his first glimpse of Bet's eyes gleaming in the trees made him startle and whirl around several times when a log popped in the crackling fire. He was grateful when several of the boys he had not met the night before came over and got breakfast ready. They showed him how to spread the fire out so that they could set up a massive iron plate over it on a clever contraption of iron legs. The boys seemed to sense his need for conversation, or perhaps it was their custom, but either way, they talked him through every move they made as they cracked eggs and stirred flour and milk together and made a hearty breakfast of thin cakes. Olifur watched this process attentively, his stomach gurgling as the scents of warm food reached his nose.

Someone rang a large bell hanging from a branch when all was ready and the boys came careening to the fire from every direction. Fritjof himself also appeared, with Bet at his heel. A tingle of fear shot through Olifur at the sight of the malkyn, but it was the pleasant sort of fear, not the abject terror he had experienced the first time he saw her.

The thin cakes were sweet and light, and Olifur ate six of them before his stomach stopped complaining of its emptiness.

After they had broken their fast, Fritjof came over to sit next to Olifur. The man sat and watched with an intense sort of silence as the boy stirred up the coals and brought an armful of branches to help build the fire back up. Fritjof did not speak for a long time. But his silence was easy and pleasant, and Olifur found that he did not mind.

At length, Fritjof cleared his throat. "You're a quick study."

A warm glow at the praise in the man's tone flooded through Olifur, even though he didn't quite understand the sentiment. Fritjof spoke in strange, clipped phrases.

Another long, comfortable silence passed between them.

"Sten! Come tend the fire for a bit," Fritjof suddenly barked.

A tall rail-thin boy bounded over, teeth gleaming in a bright smile. He tousled Olifur's hair and took the stirring stick from his hand with a gentle motion.

Fritjof beckoned at Olifur. "Come along, then."

Bewildered, Olifur followed the man to one side of the glen, where the man pulled a heavy tarp away from a long box. Inside the box lay a pile of long, straight branches that looked like staffs. Fritjof gestured.

"Choose one."

Olifur stared at the staffs in confusion, not sure what he was supposed to be looking for. "Why?"

Fritjof grinned. "I told you that you'd start making your first bow today. These are bow staves. The lads and I like to keep a supply of seasoned staves in here. You never know when you'll need to make a new bow in a hurry."

"Seasoned?" Olifur stared at the sticks, imagining the boys taking turns coming over and sprinkling salt on the branches.

Fritjof's eyes crinkled at the corners. "Just a fancy word for letting 'em sit for about a year."

"A whole year?" Olifur felt overwhelmed at the idea of such foresight.

"Aye. Fresh wood is wet wood. Snaps easier. Dry wood makes stronger bows. Letting the staves sit protected like this for a year dries them out. When we take one out, we find a new one and put it in. That'll be one of your jobs later today."

Olifur stared at the lengths of wood. He reached down and picked one that looked a little on the smaller, thinner side. Fritjof nodded in satisfaction.

"Good choice. Stand still." He took the stave from Olifur and set one end on the ground. "Come on over here and touch it with your nose. You're a little mite, so I'll cut this one down for you."

Olifur did as he was told and Fritjof made a mark on the stave with a piece of coal about level with Olifur's left eyebrow.

"There. Come."

Fritjof placed Olifur's selection on a low table. Taking his hatchet from his belt, he made a swift motion and chopped the bow stave clear through at the mark with a single blow. Then he handed Olifur the stave and the piece of charcoal.

"First thing you must do is mark all the knots."

"The knots?" Olifur stared at the implements in his hands, trying to figure out what was expected of him.

Fritjof took the other section of wood that he had removed and showed him, pointing out the knots. Once Olifur understood, Fritjof nodded and let him work. In a few minutes, he had found them all and circled them.

Next, Fritjof pulled out a slate and a small piece of pencil and showed Olifur how to sketch the shape that the bow should be.

"Ideally," he said, "we would draw this on paper and use it as a pattern, but we don't have that luxury. So you'll have to be careful as you make your cuts."

Handing the hatchet to the boy, Fritjof guided his hands along the stave in short, shallow strokes.

"Patience," he cautioned.

Together, they worked the wood into the correct shape. Slowly and steadily, until Olifur's back and shoulders ached and his hands had sprouted blisters. His arms shook as the bright, but still cool, Paute sun gleamed down on the clearing, caressing the backs of their heads. When the bell rang, Fritjof eased the tools out of Olifur's hands.

"Rest," he said, his tone low.

Olifur stepped away from the table, rolling his shoulders and stretching out his stiff muscles, and almost tripped over Bet, who had sprawled behind them in a patch of sunshine, unnoticed. He stumbled, toppling onto his back where he stared up into the fierce, wild face of the malkyn. She blinked at him, her mouth opening in a wide yawn that displayed all her sharp teeth. Then she nosed at his knee, her giant tongue peeking out to lick at him experimentally. Olifur lay on the ground, frozen.

"What do you think of our newest addition, eh, Bet?" Fritjof asked, stretching his arms as he walked over and rubbed the giant cat behind one ear. He reached down and pulled Olifur to his feet. "She'll not harm you, lad."

Olifur gave a shaky nod.

Without a word, Fritjof took his hand firmly and guided it up to pat the creature. Olifur's fingers sank into fur softer than anything he had ever imagined. He ran his fingers along her side, gaining confidence as she lay quietly beneath his caress. The malkyn closed her eyes and a deep rumble grew in her body, a vibration that startled him and made him take a step back.

Fritjof's eyes laughed at him. "She's just enjoying it, lad."

Olifur nodded and tentatively put his hand out once more.

"Lunch," Fritjof said suddenly, leading the boy back to the fire where the others had already assembled.

Olifur piled his plate high with slices of meat and small, twisty carrots. He found Kellen and Lorcan and sat between them, devouring his food with an appetite born of hard work.

After lunch, Olifur hoped to return to his bow, but Fritjof gave him a stern head shake and pointed at the fire before beckoning to several of the other boys and disappearing with them into the forest.

Disheartened, Olifur poked at the coals, keeping them alive for the rest of the afternoon. At twilight, Fritjof and the hunters returned with a massive boar dragging behind them. The whole camp erupted into a frenzy of activity and in short order the boar was prepared and hanging over the fire on a spit. Olifur watched it all with eager interest, trying to memorize every move so that he could help next time.

"Nice job with the fire today, Olifur. You are working hard. Fitting in. Fitting in," Lorcan commented as the boar crackled and smoked. Olifur swelled with pride at the older boy's words.

That night, Olifur toppled into his hammock, aching and sore and content. His hammock swayed in the gleam of starlight. In the darkness, with the comforting crackle of the fire soothing him to sleep, Olifur's thoughts turned to his parents. He pictured Mother's face, so sweet and framed in her halo of golden curls, her blue eyes filled with love; he remembered his father's strong arms lifting him up, swinging him onto his broad shoulders. Tears flooded his eyes as he thought of all he had lost, and a fierce ache grew in his chest. A cool breeze caressed his face and Olifur softly cried himself to sleep.

5

LIFE IN THE GLEN

The days fell into a steady rhythm. The rains of Urin had done their job and now the forest flourished with life and color as Paute marched by. Every day brought new colors and brighter greens until the entire wood had come completely alive. Olifur tended the fire in the mornings and evenings and helped with the dishes after every meal. The afternoons were filled with Fritjof teaching him how to craft his stave, shaping and scraping and working the wood until it had become the bow he desired. They worked slowly and carefully, only taking off a tiny amount of wood at a time. Fritjof spoke little, just enough to give him directions. Olifur often grew impatient as he watched the other boys get to go into the forest with Fritjof. He longed to be taken on those hunting trips, rather than just help with the fire and the dishes. But even though Fritjof never said anything about it, Olifur knew with certainty that if he rushed and ruined the stave, he would not be given another for a long while. So he followed Fritjof's quiet instructions and forced himself to be patient, performing each direction with slow care.

One day, after Olifur had been living in the glen for just over one lunat, the cooler days of Paute dissolving into the warmer ones of Avar, Fritjof left the clearing before breakfast. Olifur just caught a fleeting glimpse of the older man riding away on Bet. Olifur rolled out of his hammock and stumbled over to the fire, which had gone out during the night. Yawning, Olifur gathered the tinder and started a blaze going, then he began gathering up the various items for breakfast. The barrel of flour only had a few scoops left in it, but there was enough for the small cakes they usually had for breakfast. Carefully, he measured out the ingredients. He did not have the strength to lift the iron table over the fire, but he could get everything ready for the older boys.

Kellen joined him, yawning and stretching.

"Fritjof left already," Olifur said. "By himself." He tried not to let his concern show, not wanting his friend to see how much this change in the routine bothered him.

Kellen shrugged.

"Do you know where he went?" Olifur asked.

"Sure," Kellen replied, as several of the older boys joined them and arranged the skillet over the fire. "He's gone to town."

"Town?" Olifur asked.

Kellen nodded. "Where did you think the flour and eggs came from? We're not farmers."

"Does he steal them?" Olifur asked, suddenly aghast at the idea that he had fallen in with a friendly group of bandits.

The boys nearby barked with laughter at this, and Olifur felt his face grow warm. Tears sprang to his eyes, but before they could fall, Lorcan was there, a friendly arm around Olifur's shoulder.

"Nobody in this camp is a thief. No thieves. No stealing," the older boy told him in a serious tone.

Bellamie, the oldest of them, piped in. "You haven't gotten into the business side of our enterprise yet, but that's because you're still learning. We hunt and live off the land as much as we can, but we also make things. Leather pouches, extra bows, belts, all sorts of things. Fritjof takes what we make into town to trade for the things we can't get on our own. He also does work for the villagers sometimes if they need him, fixing roofs and plows, things like that. He'll be back tonight, and it'll be just like a Harvest Festival with all the things he'll have Bet loaded down with; just wait and see."

"Did he go all the way to Melar?" Olifur wanted to know.

"Probably not," Bellamie replied. "Sometimes he will, if they don't have anything to trade in Elbian. Usually he just goes to Elbian because it's closer and they know us better there. But Fritjof's name carries weight even in Melar. Several of the older boys have gone there to get good jobs once they're old enough."

"Elbian," Lorcan said knowingly. "Elbian is where he went. Where he went. He'll be back soon. You'll see. You'll see."

Olifur nodded, feeling relieved. He had gotten used to Lorcan's strange way of repeating himself. The hole where his parents ought to be still ached, but not as much. The work and the easy camaraderie of the other boys was slowly healing the hurt in his heart. And yet Fritjof's disappearance had brought back that coiled snake of fear, and though the other boys did not seem concerned, Olifur could not help himself and throughout the day he often found himself turning to stare off in the direction the man had gone.

The day proceeded slowly, but with a tinge of excitement that was nearly visible glittering in the air. All the boys went about their work with one eye to the east, hoping to catch the first glimpse of Fritjof returning.

But Fritjof did not return. The boys finished their chores. Since Olifur did not want to touch his bow without Fritjof there to guide him, Lorcan showed Olifur how to make arrows, teaching him how to find the straightest sticks possible and then how to heat them over hot coals to remove any bends from them, careful not to scorch or burn them. Once they had accumulated a good number of shafts, the two boys went hunting in the woods for feathers and suitable stones for fletching and arrowheads until the shadows grew long and the bell rang, calling them for dinner.

The last bites of watery stew had been consumed and night had arrived in all its jeweled darkness. But still, Fritjof had not returned. The boys lingered about the fire. Nobody wanted to go to sleep with excited anticipation still thick in the air. Some of the older boys began telling stories of the treasures Fritjof had brought them in the past, and Olifur remembered all the best days with his parents, times when his father had returned home from a long trip bearing special gifts, or the times when they had gone on picnics together and his parents had told him stories. The memories warmed him with a confusion of emotions: grief and joy all mixed in a strange tangle.

Olifur worried about Fritjof. Surely the old man could take care of himself on the road? Surely Bet wouldn't let anything happen to him. Bandits were swift and brutal; no one knew that better than Olifur, but Fritjof would have nothing they wanted. Surely Bet would protect him. The other boys did not seem worried, so Olifur tried to relax and let their confidence in Fritjof's eventual return seep into his own thoughts. Slowly, he let the warmth of the fire, the gentle hum of the stories, the exhaustion of the day, and his confusing emotions lull him into a doze as he sat there on the ground, his back against the log. His eyes drooped shut.

Something that sounded like thunder startled him awake. Olifur blinked his eyes in the smoky darkness, wondering why everyone was shouting. Then he felt himself being jostled as the other boys rushed around him and he came fully awake.

Fritjof had returned. Bet pulled a little cart behind her, filled to the brim with wonder. Two enormous barrels of flour, dozens of eggs and glass bottles of milk for them to put in the little box that Fritjof had helped them construct that sat in the nearby cool spring just under the surface of the water. He had lengths of canvas they could sew and stretch across tree branches to create a large tent when the rainy season returned, as well as new bundles of thatch for the cabin roof. Each boy got a rough tunic, a pair of canvas trousers, and a new knit blanket. There were knives and hatchets in among the packages, as well as a canister of precious salt. There were new water skins for them, and each boy got a tiny square of hard candy. Fritjof's eyes crinkled at the corners in response to the exclamations over all the treasures.

Then the boys took him around the camp and showed him all the things they had done in his absence. Olifur proudly showed off his arrows, and Fritjof gave him a nod and said they would start working on his bowstring in the morning. Then he shuffled them all off to their hammocks and told them if they hustled off to bed, he would tell them a story about the Builder.

Safe and content once more, Olifur climbed up the tree to reach his hammock, which Lorcan had recently helped him move up. He snuggled under his new blanket and pulled his worn elephant into his arms. It was the only thing he had left of his old life except memories; with a deep sigh, he buried his nose in its familiar scent and drifted off to sleep, listening to Fritjof's voice.

In the morning, just as promised, Fritjof began teaching Olifur the process of extracting and drying sinew to create a bowstring. Once Olifur grasped the process of where the sinew came from, Fritjof revealed a stash of already dried fibers, and they began the arduous process of creating the bowstring from them. Fritjof taught him how to chew the fibers until they had softened enough to work with and be sticky, and how to then braid them together, adding new fibers when he ran out until he had one long, continuous string. It took Olifur all morning to create the string, with Fritjof keeping a watchful eye on his progress. His fingers felt clumsy as he tried to wind the fibers together. They did not want to stick together the way they should, and he found his braid growing too loose and falling apart. Fritjof never scolded or stepped in to take over; he just grunted or muttered a suggestion until Olifur finally caught the rhythm of the motions.

It took him three full days to make the bowstring, his small fingers tripping over the work and getting sticky with the glue oozing out of the sinew. But when he had finished, Olifur felt a sense of accomplishment that he had done the work all himself.

When the string was complete, Fritjof let him cut the notches at the top and bottom of the bow and taught him how to tie the proper knots. Olifur stared at the completed bow, eager to draw it back and shoot something, but Fritjof stopped him short with a swift shake of his head.

"Not yet," he cautioned. "It's not finished."

Taking the bow, Fritjof showed Olifur how to bend it a little at a time, making sure to take note where the two halves of the bow did not match or bend equally. Together, they removed the string and shaved off little tiny bits of the bow here and there, smoothing and shaping and training the wood into the form it needed to become an effective tool.

When they had shaved the limbs until they bent nearly equally, Fritjof finally gave a nod of approval. Then he handed Olifur an old corncob and directed him to rub it over the wood until the entire stave felt smooth and gleamed as though polished. Olifur sat and worked at this job for two days before Fritjof told him he could stop. Then he gave him a can of bear grease and a cloth and made him rub the grease all over the stave.

"This will protect your bow from water," Fritjof said.

Finally, the bow was ready. They bound the grip with strips of leather, secured with more sinew, and then Fritjof had Olifur restring the bow. The older man retrieved his own bow and then beckoned for the boy to follow as he marched into the woods.

"Bring arrows," he said.

Grabbing up his stack of arrows and holding his bow carefully, Olifur trotted after the older man, his stomach leaping with butterflies of excitement.

Just inside the first line of trees, Fritjof paused and showed Olifur the targets he had marked out. They were close, just about twenty paces away.

"You'll shoot farther with practice," Fritjof explained. "But this will do for now."

He showed Olifur how to stand and how to hold his arms as he drew the bowstring back to his face with three fingers, not pinching the string, just holding it loosely at his fingertips.

Olifur gritted his teeth as he drew the string back to the

corner of his mouth. Fritjof tapped his elbow, indicating that he needed to raise it.

"Sight along the arrow," Fritjof said. "Take your time. Breathe. Release."

By the time he released the string, Olifur's arm was shaking with the effort and the arrow wobbled wildly through the air before plunging into the soft earth, nowhere near the target. The string slapped Olifur's forearm so hard it brought tears to his eyes and he yelped, but he did not drop the precious bow. Fritjof handed him another arrow without a word.

Scared of the bowstring, now, Olifur tried to hold the bow so that his forearm would not get slapped. The arrow went straight up in the air, and the string snapped against his arm even harder than before. This time, he could not prevent the tears from streaming down his cheeks. The inside of his forearm blazed bright red.

"Adjust your grip," Fritjof said. He took up his own bow and showed Olifur how to rotate his wrist just slightly to protect himself from the slapping of the string.

Olifur studied the man's movements and tried to imitate them. This time, when he released the arrow, the string did not hit his arm. The arrow sped toward the target, but without any power behind it, the arrow hit the board and bounced off, falling to the ground. Discouragement threatened to overwhelm Olifur. The pride he had felt in finishing his bow had dwindled into nothing more than a stinging sense of embarrassment. Fritjof put a hand on the boy's shoulder and held his gaze.

"You have already learned patience in making your bow," he said gruffly. "It only takes that same patience to learn how to use what you have created."

Feeling mildly encouraged, Olifur tried again, and this time the arrow stuck into the corner of the board, dangling briefly before falling to the ground.

"Already, you improve," Fritjof said. "Each morning after

breakfast, you will come here and practice. When you are ready, you will join me on the hunt."

After ten more shots, during which the bowstring snapped against his arm a total of three more times, Fritjof told him to stop.

"Your muscles will grow," he said. "But for now, it is time for your other chores."

6

TIMES OF JOY

The angry red and purple welts on Olifur's arm slowly healed, and his muscles grew stronger the more he practiced with his bow. He learned how to hold the bow to protect his forearm. His aim improved with his strength, and after several lunats of practice, he could hit the target every time, though not always near the center. However, when he remembered how his first arrows had bounced off the target, he felt good about how far he had come.

The days flew by in a flurry of activity and learning. The full moon died to a sliver, winked out, and then grew once more as the warm days of Avar lengthened into the full heat of Mirad. Another turning of the moon heralded the lunat of Avest. Olifur's body grew lean and hard. He clambered up trees and moved up into one of the high hammocks. It was a rough life, full of difficulties and hard work that Olifur had never experienced in the first seven years of his existence, but there were also times of fun and play punctuated by evenings of cozy comfort around the fire. There were wild tales and stories from the other boys, and occasionally Fritjof could be cajoled into telling a chilling story of one of his near escapes on the hunt, or some of his adventures as a boy. Olifur enjoyed the easy camaraderie with the other boys, but his favorite times were when he got to sit with Fritjof at the work-table as they crafted and fashioned various items to take to the village. These times were precious to Olifur, as they simply sat and worked together in silence. They did not need to speak. The silence between them enveloped him in comfort and peace. He found that in the days, sennights, and lunats that he had spent in the glen, he had grown to love Fritjof like a father, and the other boys had all become like the brothers he would have gladly chosen. And though Fritjof continued to be gruff and a man of few words, Olifur loved him all the more for the few times he did speak. Memories of his old life before the glen grew fainter, and he no longer cried himself to sleep in his hammock each night.

The changing colors of the leaves in the lunat of Felling brought more hunting and more work as the boys gathered in nuts and berries and stored away smoked meat for the cold, rainy season when the growing things would be scarce and the animals would be hiding away to sleep until new growth turned the land green once more. As the days grew shorter, and the colors of the trees more brilliant, Chanjar and the new year crept over them, all unawares. There was no celebration of the event, they simply moved from one day to the next, the monument passing unno-ticed. Olifur ached to be included on the hunting trips, but when-ever Fritjof came to watch him shoot, the older man would just narrow his eyes and say, "Patience." Or he might mutter for Olifur to keep practicing after he showed him a few ways to adjust his aim. They also spent many long sennights working the lengths of canvas into a suitable shelter that they would use once the rainy season drew closer.

And now the days were shorter and darker. The chillier nights brought the inhabitants of the glen closer to the fire for more frequent stories. They huddled inside the scant shelter of the cabin when it grew too wet or too cold, wrapped in their blankets and wearing every article of clothing they owned. Thankfully, the winters in this part of Turrim never resulted in much more than a thin layer of frost.

Fritjof spent long hours tramping through the forest by himself, now. The older boys said that he hated to be cooped up in the cabin, and now his foraging took him away more and more frequently. After a particularly wet season, Fritjof went on a trek where he was gone for several days. He eventually returned to the glen, soaked through and wracked with shivers. For days afterward, he barked constantly with a wet, horrible cough that seemed like it might last forever. Olifur and the other boys tended to their mentor diligently, boiling him teas and broths and keeping him covered in blankets, going without themselves so that he might be warm. Fritjof complained gruffly—but feebly—that there was nothing to worry about and that they should all just leave him alone, but the cough lingered despite his protests. It was hard to listen to him, especially at night, when there seemed to be no relief.

However, as the lunats crawled by, warmer weather returned. And when spring finally began to turn the trees green once more, Fritjof's coughing fits dissipated and soon faded from memory.

Days marched past, each one much like the last, as the seasons turned and repeated and turned again. Another year crawled by, uneventful and brimful of all the necessary activities that kept them alive and fed. Olifur felt that every hour he spent in Fritjof's Glen brought him new lessons and skills. Having proved himself with the crafting of his bow, Fritjof allowed Olifur into the full rotation of chores. In addition to tending the fire, he now helped chop and stack their firewood, and learned how to cook their meals. He learned to clean and dress game and how to smoke the meat. Along with the other boys, he raced through the forest, learning what plants were good for eating and which to avoid. He spent long afternoons fishing in the river and learning to swim. He learned how to tan animal skins and how to work the leather into bags and belts and clothes. His fingers grew nimble with the work, using Fritjof's tools to etch clever designs into his projects, and soon his work was in high demand in the village. The only thing denied him were the hunting trips.

Olifur found himself feeling more and more at home with each passing day until he could barely remember what life had been like before he came to Fritjof's Glen. Winter came and went a second time. Fritjof's cough returned, but it did not linger or seem to last as long. As spring bloomed with flowers and the forest once again adorned herself in emerald hues and Fritjof's health appeared to remain good, the worry that the boys had all been subconsciously nurturing faded.

Olifur continued to practice his archery every dry day they had, and as the warmer days returned in his third year with Fritjof and his adopted family, he finally began to enjoy the results of his patience and practice. His aim improved. His arms and grip had grown strong, and now he could send the arrow flying near the center of the target every time. As his skill grew, he joined the other boys in shooting at targets farther away and smaller, and their competitions were some of his favorite parts of each day. But still, he longed for the day Fritjof would take him hunting. It seemed like a monumental thing, and it loomed in his thoughts constantly. He anticipated that moment when Fritjof would make eye-contact and give a jerk of his head, welcoming Olifur to join him in the hunt. On that day, Olifur knew, he would become a man, fully grown and proud in stature in their little community.

His second summer sped by, filled to the brim with all the activity and beauty they could stand, and yet, to Olifur, the days were too short, too fleeting. His ninth birthday approached and passed unnoticed; nobody in the glen celebrated birthdays. The boys in Fritjof's Glen took no notice of dates in general, only of seasons. They were not the same seasons that those in the villages and farms marked, however. For the boys in Fritjof's school, there was berry-picking season, and honey-gathering season. Nut-collecting season was one of Olifur's favorites, and weeding-the-vegetable-garden season was his least favorite. Harvesting their potatoes and carrots and beans always held equal measures of fun and drudgery; it was exciting to pull up the vegetables and see how they had grown, but after a few days of that, the work turned

tedious and his fingers ached and he longed for them to be clean
and not caked with dirt. But always, his thoughts returned to
Fritjof and the hope of that promised day.

Hunting and fishing were year-round activities, even on the
coldest days of Darkthen and Edrian, when the edges of the little
stream sometimes grew a thin ridge of ice. It never became too
cold, and they rarely got snow, but it rained often in the winter,
and there were days when the air turned bitter at night.

One morning, late in Olifur's third winter in the glen, on a
day that was overcast but dry, the air held lingering remnants of
warmth, but a crisp bite to the air promised snow. Fritjof came to
watch the boys' latest archery contest. He observed silently, giving
no outward sign of his thoughts as each boy showed off his skill
and tried to impress their teacher. When they had finished, Fritjof
gave a nod, and then pointed at Olifur.

"Tomorrow, if the weather allows, we will hunt."

Fritjof turned and tromped away before Olifur could even
reply. But his heart swelled with pride at finally having earned this
highest of honors. He felt as though he might burst out of his skin
as the joy of this pinnacle of achievement filled him to overflow-
ing. Kellen, understanding his friend's beaming excitement,
slapped him on the shoulder with a hearty congratulation.

Olifur could hardly sleep that night as he anticipated the
coming hunt. He tossed and turned and finally drifted off, only to
wake again just as the horizon grew light once more. He strained
his eyes up at the sky, trying to determine if the weather would
hold for the hunt and hoping against hope that it would. Unable
to lie still in his hammock for a single minute longer, he scrambled
down the tree, careful not to make any sound that might disturb
the others. The air held a faint chill and he could see his breath
billowing out in little clouds, so he fed the fire, as long habit had
taught him to do even if it wasn't his current assignment. Then he
got himself a stick of dried meat and an apple and sat against a log,
munching and waiting for Fritjof. Some few of the earliest flowers

had poked their yellow, bell-like heads up through the patchy snow, indicating that spring was on its way.

Bet sidled up to him, her large presence warm and comforting as she curled up at his side. He snuggled into her soft fur and shared some of his meat. She licked appreciatively at his hands while he popped the remnants of the apple core into his mouth.

Fritjof appeared, silent as a spirit, the corners of his eyes crinkling in the dim predawn light. He had a large bundle strapped to his back, along with his quiver and his bow. Olifur scrambled to his feet and retrieved his own bow and a quiver full of arrows before he followed Fritjof into the forest. Bet paced at their side, a silent shadow, and Olifur grinned a little, remembering how she used to terrify him.

As they delved ever deeper into the wilderness, passing through the trees, stealthily scaling hills and traversing gullies, Olifur felt the heat of all the words he wanted to say burning in his mouth like fire. He kept them inside, knowing he must remain silent as they hunted. Fritjof would not scold him for speaking, but he would disapprove, in that quiet way he had, and Olifur knew he would forfeit future hunting trips for a long while until Fritjof felt he had once again learned the correct amount of patience. He had waited too long for this activity to lose it again in a foolish burst of emotion.

But as they hiked in silent companionship, Olifur hoped the man knew how grateful he was. Someday, he would find a way to tell him.

The exercise warmed him, and the rising sun also warmed the air slightly. But when they found a spot on a rocky ledge of a hill where they could sit and watch the surrounding area, Olifur was glad he had brought his blanket. He wrapped it around his shoulders and huddled next to Bet, trying to soak in some of her warmth. It was a suitable spot to be if any game happened by. Fritjof silently handed Olifur a leather bag full of nuts and dried berries, which the boy gratefully ate. The long trek had made him hungrier than he realized. He drank from the water skin, careful not to make gulping noises.

Together, they sat and waited. Olifur slid his fingers up and down one of his arrows, playing absently with the fletching. Bet stayed with them for a while, but then she leaped up and disappeared, probably to do a little hunting of her own.

The day wore on. Olifur got a chance at a pheasant, which he missed, but he brought down several squirrels before a good-sized buck paced into view. Olifur caught Fritjof's eye. The older man gave a slow nod, and they drew and released as one, their twin arrows singing through the air. The buck gave a great leap away, too late, before falling to the ground and moving no more.

The hunters retrieved their quarry, cleaning and dressing the meat with swift precision as the shadows grew long around them. The sun had fallen deep into the trees as Fritjof unfolded the pack he had been carrying, and Olifur was astonished to see that it was a small sledge. Together, they strapped their prizes to the sledge and Fritjof tied on the harness before turning and dragging it behind them.

"You did well," he said, breaking the spell of silence that had held them in its grip all day.

Olifur beamed at the praise as he trotted along beside the man. Happiness brimmed within him and threatened to spill over. He could not remember the last time he had felt so completely content, so full of joy.

Bet returned, bounding alongside them and nuzzling Olifur's arm affectionately, nearly knocking him over. He chuckled and scratched behind her ears, then pushed her away and followed Fritjof as they continued through the forest, backtracking the way they had come. As they made their way through a valley with steep hills climbing up on either side, Olifur thought of how beautiful everything was in the misty purple of dusk. The silence that had hung between them all day was now broken by the swishing sounds of the sledge dragging behind, and Olifur knew he could speak if he wished and say the things he had wanted so badly to say. And yet he held his peace for a while longer, savoring the silence. Today, here, on this hunt, he had begun to understand Fritjof's silence. The old man was not averse to words, Olifur realized, he just understood their value. He wanted to learn that same understanding. To say what he meant with precision and care. Not to waste his time with useless words. And so he waited, thinking over exactly what he wanted to say and how he wanted to say it.

"Fritjof," he said finally, panting under the weight of the smaller game hanging from his own pack. "I wanted to tell you…"

Before he could say another word, a scream resounded in the darkening woods, sending a chill racing up Olifur's spine. Fritjof stopped, making a motion with his hand that told Olifur to be silent, not that he needed the direction. His tongue felt frozen in his mouth and he knew he couldn't have spoken even if he wanted to.

7

GRYMSTALKER

Bet snarled deep in her throat, her body held in a stiff, defensive pose, her soft fur bristling. Olifur crouched, shaking and terrified as the scream of the grymstalker echoed through the darkness. It shattered the stillness of the forest, like breaking glass skittering through the trees. Birds awoke with loud squawks and lurched into the sky, speeding away from the feral, predatory promise held in that cry.

Fritjof slowly reached up to his chest, his fingers working at the straps of the sledge, carefully undoing the knots. He gestured at Olifur with a jerk of his chin, and the boy fumbled with his bow, nocking an arrow and holding it ready with shaking hands. Bet tensed. Her eyes gleamed in the misty twilight as the challenge of her feral cousin resounded through the woods once more.

"It just wants the deer," Fritjof hissed. "If I can get these knots undone..."

A shadow fell over them and Fritjof shouted as the leaping grymstalker's full weight knocked him to the ground. Bet snarled and attacked, knocking the grymstalker off of Fritjof, and the two enormous cats tumbled across the ground before righting themselves. They screamed and clawed at each other, their huge paws swiping at each other with terrible claws extended. Fritjof lay on the ground, still struggling with the straps, trying to get away. Olifur stood frozen, paralyzed with fear as his worst nightmare came to life before his eyes.

"Olifur!" Fritjof yelled. "Your bow!"

With trembling hands, Olifur raised his bow. Numbly, he nocked an arrow and drew in one smooth motion, his muscles taking over even as his entire mind went blank with terror. He sighted along the arrow, taking his time, breathing deep, but then he hesitated, not sure what to do.

The malkyn and the grymstalker pounced and whirled, claws flashing, snarls and screams erupting from their throats. In the darkness, Olifur could not tell the creatures apart, and he hesitated, not wanting to hit Bet. He held the drawn bow for another heartbeat, then lowered it.

"What are you doing?" Fritjof growled as Olifur knelt beside him.

"Bet's keeping the grymstalker busy. I can't get a clean shot," Olifur said, gritting his teeth to keep them from clattering together and betraying his fear. "We've got to get you out of this harness."

Squinting in the murky shadows of oncoming night, Olifur's nimble fingers picked at the knots, loosening them until Fritjof could scramble out of the harness. Stumbling as they ran, they clambered up one side of the ravine. Fritjof stopped to rest, looking down at the fight still raging. Unslinging his own bow, he nocked an arrow, training it on the two battling creatures with steady hands.

Olifur held his breath. What if Fritjof hit Bet? Time seemed to stop. The only sounds were those of the screaming cats, the only movement down in the shallow ravine below them. Olifur's every breath sounded deafening in his own ears.

And then Fritjof released the arrow.

It sped straight and true, thudding into the side of one of the whirling dervishes. The creature sprang straight into the air, and then fell to the ground, its feet moving as it dashed to get away. It climbed straight up the cliffs on the other side of the ravine, then stopped and slid back down to the floor of the ravine, dead.

Olifur held his breath, straining his eyes. Which one had Fritjof killed? He hoped it had been the grymstalker, and not Bet.

The remaining figure took a few limping steps, then sat on the ground, calmly licking one paw. It ignored the meat lying on the sledge. Fritjof gripped Olifur by the shoulder, then started back down the cliff. Olifur followed him cautiously, still not sure it was Bet down there.

But it was. She greeted them with a pitiful mewling sound, and Fritjof felt her all over, petting her and making much of her for her bravery.

"You'll get a whole pheasant all to yourself when we make it back to camp," he promised, his voice gruffer than usual. "Come on, lad."

The older man took up the sledge harness once more, and they continued on their way back to the camp. They made good time, though Olifur spent the rest of the hike dreading their return to the glen. His steps lagged and grew slower the closer they got to home. Fritjof noticed and turned to eye him.

"Did that creature take a swipe at you?" he asked, his voice full of concern. "Are you hurt?"

Olifur shook his head.

Fritjof stopped and swung around. He stared at Olifur for a long moment in the dark. "You handled yourself well, boy."

Usually, words of such high praise would have sent bursts of warmth through Olifur's very soul, but now they rang hollow.

Silence stretched between them. Olifur was glad for the darkness, that Fritjof couldn't see his face or read what was written there.

Fritjof came to stand in front of him; the sledge creaked as it dragged sideways. He laid his hands on the boy's shoulders.

"Fear is nothing to be ashamed of," he said. "Unless you let it rule you."

Something shattered inside Olifur's chest. Strangling shame

filled his throat and for a moment he couldn't breathe. "But... I... I did."

Fritjof said nothing.

Olifur hung his head. "I didn't take the shot," he choked. "I couldn't. I had my arrow ready, but..."

"Why didn't you shoot?"

The gentle question startled him and Olifur looked up, confused. He considered the question. Why hadn't he taken the shot? The moments of terror flooded back to him and he swallowed hard. "I couldn't tell which one was Bet," he said. "I didn't want to hit her."

"That doesn't sound like fear taking over," Fritjof said. "That sounds like wisdom."

Olifur frowned, his emotions a tangle of shame and confusion. He couldn't speak. Words failed to materialize.

Fritjof kept speaking. "You might have frozen for a moment," he allowed. "But you didn't let it take over. You acted. You drew your bow, but when you realized you might hurt a friend instead of your foe, you waited. Instead, you saw that you could help me, and you did. Lad, you didn't run away, nor did you stand there frozen and unable to move. You did what you could with the tools you had. Probably saved my life and Bet's with your actions."

The malkyn, hearing her name repeated, bumped her head into Olifur's chest, purring like the rumble of distant thunder as he automatically rubbed her forehead in the correct spot. "I was so afraid," he admitted.

"So was I," Fritjof muttered in a confiding tone.

In the darkness, Olifur could just barely see the man's wink. Then Fritjof swung around and continued back to the glen, leaving Olifur feeling almost whole again.

When they returned to the glen, the other boys exclaimed over the success of their hunt, and Fritjof, in rare fashion, told the story of the grymstalker attack and how Olifur's quick thinking had saved him, Bet, and the meat. The boys cheered and jostled Olifur like he was a hero, and he sat in the midst of it, feeling mildly embarrassed and more than a little deceitful. He protested their praise and told anyone who would listen how terrified he had been, but that only made them esteem him more.

Fritjof shuffled out of his overcoat, revealing deep scratches on his chest. He allowed the older boys to minister to the cuts, dressing and bandaging them, and waving away their exclamations of concern.

That night, Fritjof's cough from two winters ago returned. Olifur huddled in his bedroll near the fire and listened miserably as the man coughed and rasped. The night crawled past.

When morning finally glimmered on the horizon, Olifur threw off his blankets and stoked the fire, though it wasn't his primary job anymore. He boiled up a tea from their dried stores and took it over to Fritjof.

The man struggled to sit up and accepted the tea gratefully. He gave Olifur a weak smile. "I'll be fine, lad. My lungs have never been strong, but we have an understanding." He sipped at the tea.

"Fritjof," Olifur whispered.

Fritjof sipped at the tea until a fit of coughing overtook him again. Olifur took the tin cup while the man convulsed.

"Thank you, lad," Fritjof whispered, huddling down into his furs and closing his eyes.

"I just wanted to say thank you," Olifur said, his voice soft.

Fritjof opened one eye and peered at him. "Eh?"

"For taking me in," Olifur whispered. "After my parents..."

Fritjof reached out and gripped Olifur's shoulder. "Of course, lad. Of course. Why don't you and Kellen go hunting today?" His eyes fluttered closed again, and the man drifted off to sleep.

Olifur told Kellen that Fritjof had told him to go hunting. Kellen frowned.

"With all the meat from that buck hanging in the smokehouse? Did he say something about the weather?"

"No."

Kellen quirked his mouth. "Well, maybe he's thinking winter'll hang on a bit longer this year." The boy shrugged. "Not gonna argue with the chance to get out of camp chores. Let me get my bow!"

Kellen bounded off and was back in short order with both bows, two quivers, and a handful of dried meat that they stashed in their bags. They told Lorcan where they were heading and snagged two water skins before they left. The older boy just nodded in a distracted sort of way and waved them off as he headed to the fire to check on Fritjof.

Olifur watched him go, a thread of worry gnawing at the pit of his stomach. "You think Fritjof will be all right?"

"Sure he will," Kellen replied. "He's Fritjof, after all."

"I know, but..." Olifur trailed off.

"Come on." Kellen beckoned with a wide motion of his arm. "Fritjof's never let me be hunt leader before. Let's go before he changes his mind!"

Kellen and Olifur tramped through the woods in companionable silence. Around midday, the sun came out from behind the clouds and bathed them in its golden glow. The two boys stopped by a burbling spring and ate some of their jerky and refilled their water skins with the icy, clear water.

In the later afternoon, after bringing down two pheasants, three squirrels, and a large rabbit, they both agreed that they should turn back if they wanted to reach the glen before dark. Light snowflakes drifted down, and neither of them wished to be caught away from camp in a snowstorm. With their kills slung over their shoulders, they began the long hike home.

It had been an enjoyable day. Happiness welled up in Olifur and he and Kellen chatted as they walked, clambering over fallen trees and detouring occasionally to climb up large boulders. They each felt a deep sense of pride at what they had accomplished, and now they bounded about, no longer bothering with stealth. Olifur grinned. To be sent out on a hunt without Fritjof or one of the older boys was almost like a graduation. To be sent out on such a hunt after only one excursion was unheard of! He could hardly wait to return to the camp and show off their success.

Fritjof would be so pleased. Kellen also seemed pleased, and Olifur knew that the other boy felt just as he did. As the two youngest members of Fritjof's class, they had been granted a great honor this day.

"You're real good with that bow," Kellen commented.

"Thanks," Olifur replied. "You too."

The shadows in the forest grew longer. The boys neared the glen, chattering together about everything and nothing, when suddenly Olifur stopped. Kellen continued a few paces before he noticed his friend was no longer with him. He turned, a quizzical expression on his face.

"Something's wrong," Olifur whispered.

Kellen frowned, then cocked his head to one side, listening. "You're right," he said. "Why isn't the fire crackling? Supper should be on by now."

A sudden dread seized Olifur and squeezed. "Fritjof!" he cried, dropping everything and bursting into a run. He dashed past Kellen, breaking through the last few rows of trees, and emerged into a wholly unfamiliar scene. All the boys of the glen sat around the fire, their faces wan and gray, their expressions full of grief.

"Fritjof!" Olifur screamed again. "Fritjof! Where are you?"

Kellen caught up to Olifur and stood panting beside him. The other boy doubled over, hands on his knees, and stared at the glen.

"What happened?" Kellen asked.

Lorcan stared through them, as if unseeing. Fearing the worst, Olifur raced into the small cabin, where he paused. Fritjof lay on the small cot, his chest rising and falling with obvious effort. Bellamie sat nearby, a bowl of broth in one hand as he tried to spoon some of it into Fritjof.

"He's gotten worse," Bellamie said, noticing Olifur in the doorway. "Tell the others that we need to get the travois out and take him into Elbian to see the physician there. Pack up as many supplies as you can, and any of our craft ware that we can use to trade with the physician there. We might need to trade for lodging, as well."

"Lodging?" Olifur asked.

Bellamie ran a hand through his hair. "Yeah. I'm not sure how long we'll have to stay. There's still a lunat left of winter, at least, and it might be best if we spend it in Elbian."

Olifur frowned. "But winters here don't get too bad. And I saw flowers growing in the forest already."

"Just..." Bellamie stopped. "Look, Fritjof's cough always gets worse when it's cold. This is as bad as I've ever heard it. Just tell the others."

Olifur nodded and ran back outside, shouting orders from Bellamie at the others. Relieved at having something to do, the boys burst into action.

8

SUDDEN CHANGES

The boys of the glen hurried to make ready everything they would need for the trek into the village. Bellamie emerged from the cabin to inform them that Fritjof seemed to be breathing easier.

"I'd still prefer to leave as soon as possible, even though night's falling," he told them.

The snow continued to flurry down, and the boys packed up their belongings into carts and hitched the travois to Bet. Then they carried Fritjof outside and laid him on the drag, where they made him as comfortable as they could with blankets and furs. Lorcan led Bet along, while the other boys came behind with the carts.

Although the village was only a few miles north-east of the glen, they made slow progress, and after a few hours it became so dark that they had to pause and make camp, where they rested fitfully until the horizon ahead grew a stripe of lighter blue. By the time the sun had fully emerged from its resting place, they left the forest and crested a hill to look down on the village below. The wind swept over them, a wicked bite in its teeth, and Fritjof coughed, a dry, rasping sound that ground into Olifur's soul.

Fritjof's coughing accused him of being useless, helpless to do anything but listen.

"Come on," Bellamie said. He and Lorcan moved forward, both looking weary but determined to finish their task. The travois swished softly through the thin layer of fresh snow.

At their approach, doors opened along the main street and several townsfolk emerged from their houses, their expressions curious. At the sight of the travois, someone raced away, and by the time the boys stood in the center of the main thoroughfare, an older man hurried toward them. He had bushy white hair, and a short gray beard, not a full beard; it was more like several days of stubble due to not having enough time to shave.

"Please, sir," Bellamie began, but the man interrupted.

"The cough again?" he asked in an abrupt, no-nonsense tone. Bellamie nodded.

"Old fool. I told him to take better care of himself. Bring him." He spun on his heel and led the way, the small crowd parting for them without complaint.

Doctor Fordhras led them to a small house just a little farther down the street. He helped Lorcan and Bellamie lift Fritjof from the travois and lay him on a bed inside. The rest of the boys waited outside anxiously while the physician inspected their teacher.

Olifur sat down with his back against the wall. Bet, freed from her burden, curled up on the ground next to him. He wrapped an arm around her neck, playing with her ears and taking comfort in the gentle rumble of her purr that vibrated through his whole body. His mind drifted back to the endless hours he and his father had spent waiting on various physicians, hoping, praying.

"Dear Builder," he whispered so softly that only Bet could hear him. "Please."

It was more than an hour before Doctor Fordhras emerged from his office. The sun grew brighter as it climbed, though it did not lend any of its warmth to those below. The physician's shoulders slumped wearily as he stepped down into the street; his face had a drawn and haggard appearance to it. The boys looked up at him with eager hope, but the man spread his hands in a helpless gesture.

"I'm afraid I've done all I can for now. Fritjof's lungs have never been strong."

"Is he going to die?" Bellamie asked.

"I don't know. Keeping him indoors until winter's over will help. I've told him that, stubborn fool. You did the right thing, bringing him here."

"If he stays here for until spring, will he live?" Bellamie pressed.

"It's possible," the doctor replied. "But even so, he may never be able to return to the life he's used to. It may take skill beyond my own to restore his health."

Olifur's ears perked up at this glimmer of hope, even as the other boys stared at the ground with fixed despair. Memories sparked in his mind from years ago. Distant memories of his life before the glen. Melar had a sychstal with a renowned healer. Fritjof had said the city stood just fifteen miles away, maybe even closer, since Elbian stood somewhere between the glen and Melar. Perhaps he could find that doctor, the one who would have helped his mother. Perhaps Olifur could convince him to travel to Elbian. Of course the doctor would come. He couldn't just leave a man to die over a minor matter of a fifteen-mile journey, could he?

Thanking the Builder for his answer, Olifur quietly slipped around the corner of the house. Bet padded after him, nosing curiously at his shoulder. He paused at a cart full of supplies they had brought along and plucked up a satchel, stuffing it full of dried meat and apples. Next, he retrieved his own bow and quiver of arrows, as well as a small knife.

Fragments of half-forgotten conversations drifted into his memory. Melar was only a day away on foot. Fritjof's name carried weight there; the man had once offered to help him find an apprenticeship or a job in the city. A job would mean wages.

Wages could pay a doctor to come from the sychstal and minister to Fritjof.

Olifur's spirits lifted. "Bet, I'm going to Melar. They have a doctor there who can help Fritjof."

The malkyn butted him fondly with her head.

His mind made up, Olifur squared his shoulders and turned back the way he had come. The long journey before him was daunting, but he was no longer filled with despair as he began the long walk back to the main road. He had enough provisions in his satchel to get him to the city. After that, he would have to rely on his wits and his skills to find a good job. He whistled as he walked, his feet swishing through the wet grass. Behind him, the malkyn padded quietly. He turned to face her.

"Bet," he admonished. "You can't come with me. The city isn't a good place for you."

The enormous cat purred and rubbed against him, nearly knocking him over. Olifur relented slightly. "Well, make yourself useful then." He swung himself up on her back and leaned over her shoulders. "Just until the forest runs out, though," he said. "Then you have to stay behind."

He did not know if the animal understood, and he knew when they got closer to the city he would have to make her understand somehow, a task he did not look forward to. He could not deny that the idea of riding the cat instead of walking all that distance was appealing, and her company was a comfort. Riding her would cut the travel-time in half, and time was not his friend. He settled against her silky back and urged her forward, glad to put off for a while longer the moment when he would truly be alone. It did not cross his mind to tell the others what he planned. Fritjof had taught them to be self-sufficient, to make plans, and to take action. Trying to organize more boys going to the city would take time they did not have, and it might raise hopes only to dash them later. Neither did he think about the difficulties he might face once he reached Melar. For now, he leaned over Bet's warm back and enjoyed the feel of the wind on his face.

The malkyn's fluid lope ate up the miles between Elbian and Melar. All too soon, the forest began to thin and turn into the wide, terraced fields surrounding the city. The sun had made its entire course across the sky and Olifur decided to spend one last night outside. Better to enter the city in the morning than come ragged and tired to her gates after dark.

He found a dry hollow area beneath the roots of a giant tree and he and Bet huddled there, lending each other warmth and sharing a little of his dried meat. Curled up next to the malkyn, Olifur closed his eyes and fell asleep.

The morning sun peeking through the roots that were his makeshift roof woke him. Olifur sat up and yawned. His stomach complained, and he dug out his last handful of dried meat. Next to him, Bet rose and stretched, then butted her head against him and he shared his wealth.

The time had come.

"Bet, you have to go," he said.

The malkyn purred and nuzzled him.

"No." His voice rose. "You have to go. Go home, Bet." He spoke the words as firmly as he could. "You can't come into the city with me."

The cat eyed him suspiciously.

"Go home!" he shouted, his voice turning hoarse with emotion. "Go home, Bet! Find Kellen!"

Bet took a few steps back the way they had come. She paused, as though confused, turning back to him as though wondering why he was not accompanying her.

Olifur shook his head. "I can't. I have to go to Melar. You can't come with me. Go. Go home!" He picked up a pine cone and tossed it at her. Bet bounded away a few paces, startled. Her eyes glinted in the morning light with an accusing gleam, but Olifur set his mouth in a hard line.

"GO HOME!" he shouted, tossing another pine cone.

Shaking her head in confusion, the giant cat leaped away once more, and this time she did not stop. Her strides carried her into the trees and out of sight. Olifur stood watching the place where she had been and struggled against the sobs trying to claw their way out of him.

"I'll come home soon, Bet," he promised. "I'm sorry, but Melar isn't the place for you."

With a deep sigh, Olifur turned and exited the forest, following the road across the wide plain that made up the lowest terrace of Melar. The city itself stood high on the central terrace, surrounded by the emerald rings of its farmland. Or at least, that was what the stories said. The rings wouldn't truly turn emerald until well into spring or even summer, when the crops poked up through the dirt. For now, the land lay dormant, awaiting the farmers. Olifur trudged along the road, his heart sore with missing Bet, Kellen, Fritjof, and all the rest of his family. Tears pricked at his eyes and he wished more than anything that he could be back in the glen, working on his bow with Fritjof, or horsing about with Kellen, or learning some interesting lore about herbs and edible plants from Lorcan.

He climbed the wide, flat steppes and soon found himself at the city gates of Melar. The gates were open to travelers, and no guards seemed to be about. The morning had passed while he made his way to the city, and people bustled about along the paths. Nobody took any notice of the small, tattered newcomer. Olifur's first impression of the city was one of grime. Everywhere he looked, the remnants of winter seemed to cling to every available surface in a pervasive layer of dust and muck. Mud puddles adorned the wide pathways between small, dirty buildings. What few trees adorned the walkways were small and scrubby and leafless. He reminded himself that winter still had a hold on the land and that he shouldn't judge the place on the way it appeared, but his heart yearned for the tall trees of the forest, the cool, clear creeks, and the clean, rocky cliffs of home.

However, in order to return there, he must first endure the city and find the doctor who lived here. Olifur squared his shoulders as he saw an approaching guard. Gathering his courage, he walked up to the man.

"Excuse me, sir, but can you tell me where the sychstal is?"

The guard squinted down at him. "You sick?"

"No. A friend of mine is, though. Fritjof."

The guard frowned. "Who, now?"

"Fritjof," Olifur repeated, his spirits sinking.

"That name supposed to mean something to me?" the guard asked, not unkindly.

Crestfallen, Olifur nodded. "Fritjof said his name carried weight here."

The guard's expression softened. "It might in some quarters," he said. "But I don't know the man, myself. You said he's sick?"

"Yes." Olifur choked the word out.

The guard scratched the back of his head and pointed. "That's the road that leads to the sychstal." He eyed Olifur. "They don't work for free, you know. The physicians, I mean."

Olifur nodded. "I was hoping to get a job here in the city so I can pay a doctor to come cure my friend."

"Well. If it's work you're looking for, you might try the Platte. They're always hiring."

Olifur mulled over the man's words. It was a place to start, anyway. It would probably be better to have some money in his pocket before he went to the physicians. "Can you point me in the right direction?"

The guard eyed him. "I'm due to make my rounds past there. How about I walk you over?"

"Thank you, sir," Olifur said, falling into step next to the man.

"Name's Garth."

"I'm Olifur."

"First time in Melar?" the guard asked.

"Yes," Olifur replied.

"What do you think so far?"

Olifur hesitated, not sure he should say what he really thought. "It's big," he finally said.

Garth grinned as though he had just paid him a personal compliment. "That it is. Biggest city in Malei."

They walked in silence for a bit, until they reached an enormous building that rose into the sky higher than any building Olifur had ever seen. Unlike the rest of the structures they had passed, this building was made of solid stone and brick. A great wooden platform standing on massive iron legs ringed the top floor of the building, possibly seventy feet above the ground. Huge, ladder-like roads extended away from this platform in three directions to the north, south, and west. As Olifur stared up at it, his brain trying to make sense of what he was seeing, a shriek split the sky and an enormous contraption of brass and silver roared out from behind the building. Wheels churning high over their heads, the metal beast flew along the tracks, growing smaller and quieter as it pulled farther and farther away.

Olifur watched in stunned silence until the steaming monster had grown small in the distance, then turned to Garth, eyes wide.

"The Platte. First junction of the great train road," Garth said with an expansive gesture that seemed to take in the whole building and the road high in the air and the monster that had screamed away from them moments before all at once. "One of the great wonders of the world. Even if it is fairly new."

Olifur continued to stare.

"Quite a sight, isn't it?" The guard's voice held a considerable note of pride, and Olifur wondered if he had some personal connection to it all.

"Did you help build it?" he asked.

Garth chuckled. "No, lad. They built the train road over sixty years ago. I'm not that old! Now, see that door over on the side? That's where you can inquire about a job."

"Thank you," Olifur said, trying to impart the full measure of his gratitude to the man for taking the time to help him. "I appreciate your help."

"Think nothing of it." Garth waved. "If you ever need anything, young man, you know where to find me."

The guard turned and began walking back the way they had come, and Olifur faced the door, ready to take his first intentional steps into the future he had envisioned.

9

THE JOB

J ust inside the door, Olifur found himself staring over the top of a high desk about level with his chin. Behind the desk sat a severe-looking woman with her gray-streaked auburn hair pulled back in a tight bun. She stared down her nose at Olifur, hazel eyes sparking with annoyance.

"We don't give handouts here," she barked. "You've been misinformed. I don't know where the Daughters of the Sun are working today, but they usually have bread for orphans." She raised a sheet of paper and stared at it, effectively ending the conversation.

Olifur frowned in confusion. "Excuse me, ma'am, I think you've made a mistake..."

She lowered the paper and scowled at him. "I don't make mistakes, young vagabond. Now be off with you. I already told you I have no bread for young hooligans." She raised the paper.

"Ma'am..."

"I'll call the guards if you don't beat it!" she shrieked, half-rising from her chair and wielding the paper like a weapon.

Olifur took a step back, thoroughly alarmed. "B-but the guard brought me here!" he managed to exclaim. "He said I might find work here."

The woman paused and cocked her head to one side. "Eh?"

"I'm a ward of Fritjof," Olifur stammered desperately, hoping the woman might have heard of the man. "He once said he could get me a job in Melar if I wished." He would have continued, but the woman had set the paper down on the desk and now heaved a great sigh.

"A job. Why didn't you say so right off?" Her demeanor did not become friendly, but at least it ceased being hostile.

"I... I tried." Olifur stared at the woman, wondering what was wrong with her.

"Try harder next time," she snapped. "I don't have time for every brat that comes through that door, and most of them are lost or hungry or looking to steal things. How was I to know you were an honest boy looking for work?" Her eyes traveled up and down his form in a meaningful glare and Olifur suddenly became uncomfortably aware of his ragged and unkempt appearance. Before he could reply, however, the woman had taken up a large bell, which she swung sharply. She pointed a menacing finger at a chair off to one side. "Sit there and wait quietly. The foreman will be here to collect you. I'm too busy to go wandering around looking for him."

Obediently, Olifur took a seat. He sat quietly, back straight, toes just touching the floor. He darted a look at the woman, who had gone back to examining her papers. She noticed him watching and scowled darkly at her papers, and Olifur returned his gaze to the door across from where he sat.

Long minutes passed. He tapped his toes against the floor, which elicited a low snarling sound from the severe woman's throat. How much time did Fritjof have? Doctor Fordhras had seemed to think he might make it through the remnants of winter if he stayed indoors where it was warm. But he had also said that Fritjof's illness was beyond his ability to cure.

Olifur was just beginning to wonder if he should try to find work somewhere else, when a man with arms like tree branches barged through the door with the force of Bet tackling one of the boys to the ground. His white beard stuck out in straw-like bristles and he glared at the woman.

"What is it now, Sooki?" he demanded. "I swear, if this is another trivial matter, I will confiscate your dratted bell and you'll just have to come find me on the floor when you need something. I can't come running every time you can't reach the top shelf..."

The woman pointed coolly at Olifur, interrupting the man mid-sentence. "Young gentleman looking for a job," she said, her tone mocking. "Thought you'd want to interview him yourself, Hughin."

Hughin frowned down at the boy. "He doesn't look like much. How old are you, boy?"

Olifur rose to his feet. "Ten at my last birthday, sir."

"Got any skills?"

"I can bend a bow and hit an acorn at a hundred paces, same as any other boy from Fritjof's Glen," Olifur replied modestly. "I can trap, fish, hunt, and work leather and wood."

"Humph." Hughin scowled, unimpressed. "Can you follow orders?"

"Yes, sir."

"Got any place to stay?"

"Not yet, sir."

"Well, if you're willing to work hard and can follow orders, you can have the job," Hughin finally said. "I won't stand for any shirking or dawdling. Shifts start at dawn and end an hour after dusk. You'll work six days out of seven. Pay is five stin a sennight, less room and board, which will cost you three stin a sennight, deducted from your pay. You'll get two meals a day and a mattress on the floor in the dormitory."

Olifur nodded, doing the math in his head. Two stin for six days' work did not seem like much, but it was a place to start. He had no idea how much money he would need to convince a doctor to return with him to Elbian to cure Fritjof, but he would spend his evenings and his day off each sennight discovering that information, and he could keep an eye out for a better position. In the meantime, he would have food and shelter.

Hughin beckoned. "Follow."

Olifur trotted after the man, following him deep into the building and up seven long flights of stairs. As he jogged along to keep up with the man who did not appear to care whether or not he fell behind and got lost forever, Olifur realized that all the grime he had seen outside must call the Platte its home. Grayish soot covered every visible surface. He grimaced and felt homesick for his green glen all over again.

Hughin opened a door and ushered Olifur outside onto a wide deck that butted right up to the train road. And resting before him sat the first clean thing he had seen in Melar: the train. Olifur stared.

Painted in a pleasing combination of red and gold, the six coaches gleamed in the sunlight. Thick, red velvet curtains hung inside pristine glass windows through which Olifur glimpsed luxuriously cushioned seats. His mouth dropped open, and he took a step toward the vision.

A rough hand grabbed his collar and yanked him sideways. Olifur yelped and choked as he stumbled and nearly fell.

"Oh, no. You don't start this job working inside the train," Hughin grunted. "Owner of the Platte hand-picks only the best of the best for that duty." He eyed Olifur. "I wouldn't count on reaching so high if I was you. Come on, you'll start with tallow-works. Do a good job at that for a few years, you might get promoted to loading. Pays an extra stin every sennight."

Disappointed that he wouldn't get even a small peek inside the train, Olifur dutifully followed the man toward the back of the train. Between the last two cars, they found a small boy with a bucket clasped to his belt and a rag over one shoulder. He stepped up onto the deck as they approached.

"Aric, this here's..." Hughin squinted at Olifur. "What'd you say your name was?"

"Olifur."

"Olifur," Hughin barked. "Show him the ropes today. And when you turn in for the night, tell Devin he can move to loading. He's most senior in your group." Hughin glared down at Olifur. "Pay attention, boy, because tomorrow you do the work on your own. If you can't keep up, you're out. Understand?"

Olifur nodded.

"Good." The man charged off and disappeared through a door.

Aric gave Olifur a wary glance. "Greasing duty. It's where everybody starts. It's not too bad so long as you watch your step. You get used to the smell after a while." He raised the bucket for emphasis, then stepped back down onto the tracks. With nimble movements, Aric ducked down and edged along the outside of the train, gripping the foot rail above him with one hand. He dipped his rag into the bucket hanging at his side and, in one expert motion, slung the rag full of grease all around the axle of one wheel. He wiped away the excess and slid a few steps to the right, swiftly working on the next wheel.

Olifur leaned over and peered between the slats of the train road. Despite his experience sleeping in high swinging hammocks in the glen, the view made him feel a little dizzy and sick. One misstep, one missed grip, and a boy could easily slip through the slats and fall to his death.

Aric swung himself out from between the wheels and up onto the solid deck. He put a hand on Olifur's shoulder. "You all right? You look a little green."

Olifur shook his head. "I'm all right. I just didn't expect to be given such a dangerous job."

Aric shrugged. "The smallest of us get axle duty. It's easier for us to move around between the wheels and under the trains. Just got two rules. First one is: one hand for the bucket, one for the rail, and don't mix 'em up. And the second is: know the schedules."

"Know the schedules?" Olifur repeated, feeling lost.

"The train schedules. Wouldn't want to be underneath one of

them wheels when it suddenly started moving, neh?" The boy gave him a wicked grin. "Ah, don't look so frightened. It's mostly pretty boring. Until someone falls."

Olifur shuddered, and Aric slapped him on the back good-naturedly. "Come on, let's get you a bucket."

Olifur followed him into a large room filled with various supplies. He observed as the other boy selected a bucket, a belt, and a hook. Aric showed Olifur how to fill his bucket with the thick, yellow tallow. Then he made him practice dipping the rag into the bucket a few times to get a feel for the motion and so that he would get used to the smell.

"Don't want the fumes making you pass out while you're on the tracks," Aric joked.

Olifur was starting to think that he should look for a different job, when Aric pronounced him ready to begin on the real thing.

"You take the near side, I'll take the far," Aric said.

Olifur's stomach clenched. He followed Aric back out to the train. Carefully, he stepped out onto the tracks, hanging onto the foot rail so tightly his fingers began to feel the strain right away. He dunked the rag into the bucket and slopped it onto the nearest axle. Great yellow glops dripped down the wheel, and he grimaced as some of it splattered back at him. A few drops got into his mouth and he coughed and sputtered, trying to spit the disgusting gunk out.

Aric laughed. "Everyone does that the first time."

Olifur moved over to the next wheel, being more careful this time. Each axle took him three or four times as long as Aric, but the other boy did not offer to assist, even when he had finished and Olifur was still struggling to complete his second coach. As darkness closed in, another boy came up on the deck and carefully lit the oil lamps without greeting either Aric or Olifur. He simply did his job quietly and then left.

Finally, Olifur finished with the last axle. He stepped wearily onto the deck, his left arm and hand sore and aching. His stomach growled. He looked about, trying to find Aric, but the other boy had disappeared.

Olifur dragged himself back to the storage room and put his tools away carefully. Then he ventured down into the building in search of supper.

He followed his ears and emerged on the ground floor into a long room crammed with tables and benches. One end of the room had been partitioned off as a kitchen and held an enormous wood-burning stove upon which a black pot sat. A long counter extended across the back of the room, with a deep sink over which a hand pump delivered running water straight into the building, a luxury Olifur had only heard about but never seen.

He made his way over to the counter between the dining area and the kitchen. An emaciated woman with sunken cheeks and wispy gray hair tied back from her face eyed him impassively as he took up a bowl.

Without a word, the woman ladled a meager spoonful of the pot's contents into his bowl and handed him a dark roll. Olifur stared down at the small repast and glanced up, about to ask for a bit more, but the woman's ferocious glower warned him away. Shrugging his shoulders, Olifur took a seat at an empty table and morosely tried to break off a piece of the roll. It cracked and crumbled in his hands, scattering precious crumbs across his bowl and the table. Grimacing, Olifur sighed and crushed the remainder of the roll over his bowl and into the mushy mass. Then he spooned the mixture into his mouth and nearly gagged at the slimy texture. Thankfully the taste wasn't horrible, but the texture was approximately what he thought might happen if he boiled slugs. Grimacing, he forced a second bite into his mouth, purposing to swallow without attempting to chew. In this way, he got through the meal and found himself grateful that the woman hadn't given him a larger helping.

As he finished up the last dregs of his meal, Olifur glanced around. The dining area was nearly empty, but then he spotted

Hughin sitting at a table on the far side of the room. Olifur rose from his seat and took his bowl and spoon to the sink.

"Where do I wash my bowl?" he asked the woman.

Her brow furrowed in confusion as she stared down at him. "Eh?"

"My bowl?" Olifur waved it. "I'm finished. Where do I wash up?"

The woman stared at him in suspicious silence for a long moment. Then she jerked her head at the large sink. "Drop it in there."

Olifur frowned. He was used to washing his own dishes, and he did not like the idea of making more work for this woman, but she stared at him in such furious bewilderment that he decided not to press the issue. He carefully placed his dishes in the sink, nodded graciously at the woman with a polite "thank you," that seemed to anger her even further, and then he made his way over to where Hughin sat.

"Excuse me, sir," Olifur said, "but where do I sleep?"

Hughin slurped up a spoonful of stew and pointed at the large double doors that led to the stairs. "Third floor, last door on the left."

"Thank you," Olifur said.

The man grunted but didn't bother to look up. Olifur shrugged and made his way up to the dormitory. When he found the room, he was not surprised to find it as dark and dingy as the rest of the building. One wall had actual bunks, stacked three beds high, but most of the other beds were simple pallets arranged on the floor in tidy rows. Aric saw him enter and came bounding over to him.

"You're over there." He pointed at the far corner.

Olifur nodded and picked his way over rows of sleeping boys until he reached his own spot. He stared down at the worn and battered straw-stuffed sack that perhaps once could have been called a mattress, and wrinkled his nose. The straw smelled strongly of mold, and even in the dim light he could see that the threadbare covering was itself covered in stains.

He sat down on the mattress and stared into the darkness, but his mind kept jumping from one thing to another, racing off in a hundred directions at once. He needed to process all that had happened, and he wanted to see more of the city. Though dark had fallen, it was not yet late, and despite the long day, Olifur did not yet feel tired. Rising from the mattress, he tiptoed back across the room, down the stairs, and out into Melar.

10

THE CITY AFTER DARK

The late winter air held a hint of mist that kissed Olifur's face as he exited the Platte and stepped out onto the streets. Swinging his arms for warmth, he hurried up the street the way he had come with the guard. He passed many buildings and homes, their wooden walls and sod roofs looking dingy in the darkness. His stomach complained that he had not eaten enough, but he ignored it. He had been hungry before. Already, he had determined that he would spend his day off in the forest outside the city, where he could hunt or fish for his own food. He would eat well at least once a sennight.

For now, he wandered along the packed dirt paths until he reached the main street, a path paved with fine, loose sand. Here, tall, gleaming oil lamps lined the street. They cast a cozy glow along the way and over the various open booths that stretched out into the center of the city in a wide swath of tables and brightly colored awnings. Sweet smells from bakeries drifted in the air and Olifur raised his nose to sniff appreciatively. People walked along the streets, ducking into stores and strolling amiably with their friends and families. They passed by, not noticing the ragged urchin who stood in the shadows and watched them with hungry eyes.

Olifur drank in the sights, the sounds, the smells. His feet padded over the smooth dirt, and he let his hand trail across the cold, columned lamp posts as he passed them by. The mist on his face caused him to shiver, but it did not cause enough discomfort to chase him back to his uncomfortable bed at the Platte.

He made his way across the city, catching snatches of conversation. A baker, in a hurry to close up his shop for the night, spotted Olifur and offered him a sweet biscuit laced with oranges and cranberries in exchange for sweeping out the shop. Olifur took the job gratefully, doing so thorough of a job that the man gave him two biscuits and told him he could have the same any night he wished to make the exchange. The prices in the window for a simple biscuit informed Olifur that it might take him years to hire the doctor Fritjof so desperately needed. Discouragement weighed heavily on his soul.

Olifur thanked the man, promised to be back, and strolled on, holding the biscuits close to his face. Their scent overrode the briny stench coming from the eastern quarter, where Melar butted up to the ocean from which most of the inhabitants of the city earned their living. He bit into a biscuit and wrinkled his nose. Though the sweet-tartness of the pastry was far sight better than the stew he had endured at the Platte, the biscuit itself was stale and crusty, a thing the baker could never have sold. Even this small kindness had been given only out of self-interest. There was nothing truly beautiful or kind in this place. His heart ached with longing for home, for Fritjof and the boys who had been like a second family to him, for Bet's warm fur and the blazing stars shining down at him like crystals in a black velvet sky.

He caught sight of a stocky, broad-shouldered figure up ahead and recognized the cut of a guard's uniform. Olifur pumped his legs into a slow jog until he was close enough to see the man's face in the gaslight.

"Garth!"

The guard turned, a question in his eyes, until he caught sight of Olifur, and his broad face suddenly burst into a grin. "Olifur! How are you getting on?"

Olifur grinned up at the guard. "All right." He raised up the extra biscuit. "Want one?"

Garth's pleasant smile changed to instant suspicion and shadows. "And where did you get this, then?"

Olifur jerked his head back the way he had come. "Hildy's. Master Epps gave me two for sweeping out his shop. They're a day old."

Garth's face fell back into a smile. "Good old Master Epps. My thanks, Olifur. I was just feeling a mite hungry." He accepted the biscuit and took a bite. "A touch crusty," he agreed. "But you can't beat the flavor. Master Epps is a genius when it comes to flavor combinations. On your first day off, look me up in the morning and I'll treat you to one of his fresh goods."

Olifur nodded eagerly.

"Have you found the sychstal yet?"

Olifur shook his head and Garth offered to take him there, as it was directly in the path of his rounds. They chatted as they walked until they reached a long, low building. The wooden walls here were sturdier than most of the other buildings throughout the city, and had been freshly painted in a deep umber that stood out from the paler gray and weather-stained structures around it.

"Here we are," Garth said. "I know one of the orderlies. Come on, I'll introduce you."

Nervous anticipation jangled in the pit of Olifur's stomach as the kindly guard guided him through the front door. Inside, all was quiet. The walls inside were a pleasant shade of yellow.

"Ho, Pelyn," Garth greeted the orderly who came forward, an elderly woman dressed in a plain mint-green gown.

"Ho, Garth," she replied. "Who's that you have with you?"

"This is Olifur," Garth introduced them. "He has a sick friend he's hoping to find a physician for."

Her gaze swept over him. "Tell me about this sick friend."

Olifur poured out his story to her, telling her all about

Fritjof's recurrent cough and the things the Elbian doctor had said. "My father told me that an excellent doctor lived in Melar. We were coming here to beg him to heal my mother several years ago..." He trailed off, not wanting to relive those memories.

Pelyn pursed her lips. "That would probably be Doctor Sveljen," she said. "He is the best we have, and his name has received acclaim beyond Melar."

"How much would he charge to travel to Elbian and cure my friend?" Olifur asked, hoping the number wouldn't be too high.

Pelyn's gaze took on a distant look and her lips moved slightly as though she were calculating. After a long pause, her eyes refocused. "I can ask him when he comes in tomorrow morning, but I'd guess he wouldn't do it for less than fifty stin. Maybe as much as a bar. I don't know."

Olifur's spirits sank through the floor. Fifty stin would take him half a year to earn at the Platte. A bar would take a whole year. He didn't know how long Fritjof had, but he certainly didn't have that kind of time.

His face must have showed his distress because Pelyn's gaze softened. "Sometimes he will waive his fees," she told him. "But he'd still need at least twenty stin just to cover his travel expenses and any medicines he might use."

Olifur nodded dejectedly. It was still a lot of money. "I'll have a day off at the end of the sennight," he said. "Can I come see Doctor Sveljen then?"

"He will be here. Mornings are best if you want to talk to him before he gets too busy. I'll tell him about your friend, too."

Olifur nodded his thanks and bade both Pelyn and Garth goodnight before wandering back out onto the street. His eyelids sagged as the long day finally began to overtake him. He longed for his bed, no matter how lumpy or smelly it might be. And yet he continued to wander, urged on by some invisible force that propelled him to explore just a few minutes more. Half-forgotten memories awakened within him and he continued to travel up and down streets and around corners, searching for something he could not name. Melar had been their destination a lifetime ago when he set out in a carriage with his father and mother. This had been the shining hope in their hearts, the place where the healers could make Mother well again. Even though he was older now, and knew that such feelings were just a fairy tale, a part of Olifur had expected to find something more in its streets and doorways, a promise of something grand and healing, a balm to his soul. Perhaps that was why he had truly come. Yes, he needed to bring a doctor back to help Fritjof, but something deeper had urged him here, and now he found that all his expectations had been nothing but hollow shells.

Then he saw her.

Standing in the warm glow of one of the gas lamps, a tall, willowy figure wrapped in a ragged brown dress that fell to her feet in an uneven hem caught his gaze. Gleaming wisps of gold escaped from the headscarf she had wrapped around her in an effort to stave off the cool mist. She was bending down, offering a morsel of something to a lean and angry looking creature that might have been a dog, or perhaps a starved wolf driven into the city by desperation. Probably a dog, Olifur thought.

The creature snarled at her, but then paused, caught by the scent of whatever was in her hand.

"It's not much, little one," she soothed, her voice soft and sweet. "But you may have some."

Suspiciously, the creature eyed her. Olifur wanted to shout, to warn her. One snap of the dog's jaws could take off her hand. But instead, as he watched, the creature whined softly and nuzzled the treat gently from her fingers before scampering off down an alley, disappearing into darkness.

From the shadows of a building, Olifur stared at the woman, his eyes tracing her face from afar. She had a sweet smile on her lips, and she looked so much like his mother it made his heart ache with longing to go over to her and ask her name. Unable to overcome his awkward shyness, he remained in the shadows, distant and silent, but warmth filled his heart. Perhaps beauty and kindness did exist in this wretched place, after all.

The woman crossed the road and disappeared down a side street and the moment of light and hope ended, leaving Olifur shivering in the dark cold of a night that suddenly left him bereft. Wrapping his arms around himself, he retraced his steps back to the Platte where he wearily climbed the stairs and threw himself down onto the lumpy mattress where he slept until morning.

———

THE DAYS SETTLED into a monotonous routine. Olifur woke each day at dawn and worked until after dark, only getting brief breaks for nearly inedible meals. He did his best to avoid Hughin's glower as he soon found that the man was impossible to please. The overseer labeled even the best efforts as "laziness," and every task he inspected needed to be redone. The man often carried a cane, which he would apply with sharp raps to the head and shoulders of any boy he believed was shirking his duties.

The other boys weren't much for talking, though they seemed to have plenty of disdain for the newest member of their little tribe. After that first day, even Aric refused to speak to him, though Olifur heard plenty of whispered snickers aimed his way. He did not understand why they singled him out. His clothes were no more tattered than anyone else's, his work no slower. In fact, he worked harder and longer and with fewer complaints than the others, but none of that saved him from getting tapped just as hard or as often by Hughin's cane. And none of it saved him from the glares of his fellow workers.

On the last day of his first sennight working at the Platte, Olifur accepted his two stin from Sooki and fled the hated, ugly building, escaping through the city gates and racing down the terraced flight of fields into the open air. In the darkness, he fairly flew down the long road and dove deep into the trees of the small wood outside the city. He scaled a good-sized tree and found a wide branch on which to sleep. With the fresh air blowing softly across his face, Olifur spent a more restful night than he had in days.

In the early hours before the dawn, he retrieved his bow from where he had hidden it before he entered the city and went fishing. Over a small fire, he cooked his own breakfast and ate like a king. He would have preferred to stay out in the woods the entire day, but thoughts of Fritjof bumped around anxiously in his mind, and so he eagerly returned to the city, his feet leading him back to the sychstal, hoping to find Doctor Sveljen.

When he reached the building, he walked in confidently and asked the first person he saw if he might speak with Doctor Sveljen. The harried-looking orderly barked something at him and pointed at a door on the left. Olifur, feeling suddenly uncommonly overwhelmed, tapped timidly at the door. A deep voice bade him enter, and he pushed the door open to see a large man standing at a long counter mixing up something in a metal bowl. The man had broad shoulders and massive arms that rippled with muscles. His hair was thick and dark, and he wore a neatly trimmed thin mustache and goatee. The man looked up from his mortar and pestle and gave Olifur an encouraging smile from beneath bushy eyebrows, his blue eyes twinkling with interest and energy.

"You must be the young man that Pelyn was telling me about this morning," he boomed. "Come in. Tell me about your friend."

Olifur entered the room and stood awkwardly near the counter, feeling small and insignificant next to this giant of a man. Doctor Sveljen, seeming to sense his shyness, began asking questions, and soon Olifur was pouring out all the details he knew about Fritjof. Sveljen listened carefully, continuing to mix his mysterious ingredients. He nodded and occasionally paused his mixing to jot down a few notes in a little book of blank pages.

"And where is he now?" Sveljen unrolled a map, and Olifur

pointed to the tiny dot representing Elbian. Sveljen nodded and made another note.

"It sounds like he has dealt with this ailment for many years," he commented.

"I think so," Olifur replied.

"But when you left him, the doctor in Elbian seemed to think he was stable?"

Olifur paused. "Doctor Fordhras thought that staying indoors until it got warmer would help."

"Then not an emergency situation," the doctor muttered. He glanced up at Olifur's face, noted his expression, and said, "Not yet, anyway. Pelyn told you of my fees?"

Olifur nodded dejectedly.

"Twenty stin should about cover my expenses," Sveljen said, staring down into his bowl with a studious expression.

Olifur glanced up swiftly. Had he heard correctly? "Sir?"

"Can you manage that much?" Sveljen asked, still not looking at Olifur.

"It will take me several sennights," Olifur admitted.

"Wonderful. I will need some time to prepare what medicines I can based on your description," Sveljen replied. "But I must warn you, I might not be able to perform the miracle you're hoping for. And it might even be too late already."

"But you'll try?" Olifur asked, trying not to think about his own worries that perhaps Fritjof had already died in his absence.

"I will try my hardest," the doctor promised.

"Then I'll be back soon," Olifur said.

"One more thing." Doctor Sveljen's voice halted Olifur before he could get through the door.

"Yes?"

"How did you hear of me?"

Olifur felt his face grow warm. "Well, I... I didn't... not really."

Doctor Sveljen's eyebrows lifted, but he remained silent, waiting.

"Several years ago, my mother..." Olifur's mouth went dry. He hadn't spoken of them with anyone in so long. "She was real sick. My father tried everything. We were on our way to Melar when..." His throat tightened. "My father said there was a great doctor here." He shrugged, not wanting to say more, fighting back the tears that threatened to spill down his face at the memories.

"I see." Doctor Sveljen stared at Olifur for a long moment. Then he nodded as if to himself. "I will do all I can."

"Thank you," Olifur choked out. Then he turned and raced out of the sychstal, running all the way back to the Platte, his two stin jingling together in his pocket, their tune seeming to be one of hope and promise.

When he returned to the dormitory, nobody asked where he had been. And in the morning, the tedium resumed.

And so, the days passed. Another sennight passed. Four small, precious coins now rested safely in the little pouch he had made from a scrap of unwanted fabric. He saved his stin carefully, counting how many more sennights it would take before he could pay the doctor to come tend Fritjof, all the while praying that the Builder would keep Fritjof alive until then. Each sennight, he tucked his pay into the pouch and nestled it carefully inside a hole in his mattress. Every time he had a day off, he escaped to the forest. And every night, Olifur walked the city streets, clinging to the one spot of brightness and beauty that existed in all of Melar.

He did not find the woman every time he went out, but he glimpsed her often enough to keep him returning to his route. Sometimes he found her walking in the small park near the city's center. Sometimes he would snatch a glimpse of her walking with a tall man in a long, shabby coat, his face shadowed by a tall hat. But always, he found her smiling. And often, he found her in the act of some small kindness: handing a stin to an orphan, feeding a homeless animal, scattering seeds for the tiny birds that fluttered in the scrubby trees of the park... her compassion knew no creature too small or lowly to be worth her while.

He treasured these small glimpses of the woman, holding them close to his heart as he clung precariously to the underside of the train until his fingers ached. They cheered him in the lonely dark of the dormitory as he listened to the scurrying pitter-patter of the rats in the walls. The memory of her smile gleamed like a jewel in his mind, helping him swallow the mushy repast served in the mess hall twice daily.

When he could not find her, Olifur would return to Hildy's and sweep it out for a day-old biscuit or two. The other shoppes in the area soon learned that he was a hard worker and trustworthy, and they would sometimes offer him a stin for running an errand or doing some distasteful or menial chore. He agreed to them all. Every coin he earned held the promise of home and Fritjof's return to health.

11

THE PLATTE

Alunat passed. Winter faded away quietly like a forgotten specter, and the days began to grow warmer, giving Olifur hope that back in Elbian Fritjof would be recovering. But still he worked, determined to bring the doctor to his friend. One night, near the end of his first lunat in Melar, weary from his regular tramping around the city, Olifur returned to his pallet and immediately sensed that something was wrong. It took him a few minutes of frantic searching, but with a sinking sensation in the pit of his stomach, he realized the truth. The money he had so carefully stashed inside his mattress was gone. Disbelief shuddered through him. All nine of his carefully hoarded stin and the little pouch he had kept them in had vanished. Three whole paydays, all the work he had done at the Platte, the extra hours helping shop owners in the evenings, and his rising hope of seeing Fritjof and the others again soon flitted away like a puff of smoke. Fear at what this delay might mean for Fritjof's health seared his soul and left him paralyzed for a long, breathless moment. Then anger flashed through him, dull and orange like the hottest embers in the center of a fire. He stood up and shouted, not caring who he woke.

"Who took it?" he demanded, his voice loud and wrathful.

A general groan came from several directions as his shout roused the other boys from their sleep.

"Go to bed," someone muttered.

Olifur marched over to the speaker and grabbed him by the collar, yanking him from his mattress. "Someone stole my money," he growled.

The boy blinked blearily up at him in the dim light. "What?"

"You're the closest," Olifur said. "Did you steal my money? I need that money! You don't understand what it means!"

Other boys were rousing now, sitting up on their beds and watching with interest, like birds of prey watching two mice squabble over a crumb. Olifur glared around angrily in the moonlight pouring through the high window. Tears of rage and righteous indignation flooded his eyes.

"If you're going to keep your coins out in the open like that, you deserve to have 'em pinched," Aric's voice scoffed from an upper bunk.

Olifur whirled and advanced on the boy, craning his neck to look him in the eye. Aric must have seen something menacing in his expression because he held his arms up.

"I didn't take it," he said, waving his hands in the air. "I'm just saying, it's not like it's a secret where you keep your wages. What did you think would happen?"

Olifur deflated. Back in the glen, none of the other boys would have dreamed of stealing from one another. Their hammocks had been sacred, and anything in one boy's hammock was completely off-limits to anyone else. That had been one of Fritjof's strictest rules. The man had often preached against the wickedness of stealing, and Olifur and the other boys had taken his stern words to heart.

Now his heart ached.

Olifur's shoulders slumped, and he turned back to his bed. He could not put a name to the way he felt as he curled up on his uncomfortable mattress, but the world itself had shifted under his feet. It was as if the ground had turned into rippling waves, no longer tethered to a firmness he trusted.

He had worked so hard. He had borne up bravely under all they had piled on him, but this blow took the breath from his lungs. Everything he had striven for was gone and he must now start over. It was more than he could bear. Olifur threw himself onto his mattress and sobbed silently into his pallet until he had emptied his soul. Then, wrung out like a wet rag and weary beyond caring, he closed his eyes and fell asleep.

———

"KID, HEY, KID!"

Olifur squeezed his eyes shut, rolling away from the persistent irritation. Someone was shaking him and shouting into his ear with a voice full of urgency, but Olifur did not wish to acknowledge it. He pulled his ragged blanket up around his chin. He had determined to be done with this wretched place and all its wretched inhabitants. He would no longer give them anything of himself.

"What's his name?"

A muttered exchange.

"Olifur? Olifur! Wake up."

At the use of his name, Olifur blearily blinked one eye open. Aric bent over him, a panicked look in his eyes.

"What?" Olifur scowled.

"You're supposed to be at your shift already. Everyone's finished breakfast already and you're going to be late," Aric said.

"So? What do you care if Hughin raps me on the head with his stick?" Olifur rolled away from the other boy and closed his eyes.

"It's not you he'll beat if you're late, it's me."

Olifur frowned and rolled back over. Aric's face had gone pale. "What? Why?"

"You're part of my crew," Aric muttered, casting his gaze at the floor. "I'm responsible. If my crew isn't where it's supposed to be, I'm the one Hughin will take it out on."

"Why?" Olifur asked. This was a new revelation to him. He was used to being rapped about the head and shoulders for his own perceived faults, but never for another boy's.

Aric shrugged. "It's part of being crew leader."

A small, ugly, selfish side of Olifur wanted to ignore the older boy's plight, roll over, and go back to sleep. The other boys were all thieves and liars. What did he care if his actions brought the punishment they so justly deserved down on their heads? For just a glimmer of a heartbeat, Olifur hesitated. But then he seemed to see his mother's face hovering before his eyes, a faint tinge of sorrow to her features. And Fritjof's voice, gruff in his ears, speaking of the Builder and the way they should live and treat others.

His conscience pricking him into action, Olifur rose from his mat. He gave Aric a wry shrug and followed him up the stairs.

"Guess I missed breakfast," Olifur muttered as they climbed.

Wordlessly, Aric handed him an apple and a chunk of cheese. Olifur accepted the peace offering and his conscience smote him more.

"It really wasn't you?" Olifur asked.

Aric shook his head. "I'm not a thief. But some of the others are."

Olifur nodded, his teeth crunching into the apple.

"We all have to find good hiding places for our wages," Aric said. "I guess I should have warned you."

It was the closest thing to kind words that Olifur had heard here inside the Platte, and he wondered at it. Perhaps Aric still had a portion of his own conscience left to him.

When they reached the platform, Olifur and Aric worked side by side on one set of axles while the other three boys in their group worked on the next car down.

Feeling an unaccustomed sense of companionship for this aloof boy, Olifur tried at conversation.

"We ought to have harnesses for working up here," he said as a trial topic.

Aric barked a short laugh. "Might as well suggest that they should build the train roads on the ground."

Olifur chuckled in response. Imagine, the enormous train roads set into the dirt where bandits could attack them or their passage could be blocked by a herd of leythan! He couldn't begin to imagine all the troubles that would cause. The frustration carriage drivers would experience waiting for the long trains to speed by might cause a revolution. And consider the dangers to lone travelers who might not hear the trains in time, or might get their foot stuck crossing the roads. No, it was better for the train roads to have been built so high in the air as they were. At least he and the other boys accepted the dangers of their jobs with full understanding of them.

"What makes the trains run?" Olifur asked after another brief span of silence.

Aric shrugged one shoulder. "The cynders."

Olifur grimaced. He had occasionally glimpsed the cynder-boys transporting the glowing yellow cylinders up to the engine. "Yes," he replied. "But what are the cynders? How do they work?"

"If I knew that, do you think I'd be greasing axles for two stin a sennight?" Aric asked, his expression full of disdain.

"Nobody knows how they work," Czel said from the other side of the train. "They're magic."

"Magic don't exist," Aric scoffed.

"Me mum said they were magic," Czel insisted. "Evil magic."

"You never had a mum," Aric teased.

"Did so!" Czel shouted.

"Hang on," Olifur interjected, fearing that an argument would lead to blows or someone slipping between the tracks. "Where do the cynders come from, then?"

Aric and Czel both paused, thoughtful expressions on their faces.

At last, Aric spoke slowly. "They get brought in on carts coming up through the south gates. Always the south."

"I once overheard Hughin talking with one of the drivers about the mines in Vallei," Czel offered.

"They're mined? Like an ore?" Olifur asked.

Aric squinted, wiping his rag carefully around a wheel hub. "I guess. I'm not sure. I've seen empty cynders, and they just look like ordinary rock. I think they mine the ore, shape them into cylinders, and then... they... do something to the ore. Whatever they do, that's what turns them into cynders so they can power the trains."

"Magic," Czel reiterated, nodding firmly.

Aric looked as though he wanted to argue some more, but then he sighed. "Might as well be," he said. "For all we're ever gonna understand it."

"They're dangerous, anyway," Czel said, relenting a little. "Maybe they're not magic, but only the most careful and steady of us boys get put on cynder-transfer."

"How come?" Olifur asked, rubbing his rag into some of the harder-to-reach crannies.

Czel gave him a serious look. "They can explode if they're dropped."

Olifur laughed, sure that the other boy was teasing, but he stopped when he saw that both Czel and Aric were staring at him in horror. He exhaled in a burst.

"Oh, come on," he said. "Surely not?"

Aric nodded, his expression somber. "One time, the cart bringing a load of cynders was late. Hughin sent out some boys to investigate. They walked for ten miles before they found the cart, but all they found were splinters and a crater and a couple of badly burned and dazed leythan wandering about aimlessly."

Olifur's eyes widened. He still felt inclined to believe that Czel and Aric were joking, but their expressions held such deadly seriousness that he could not bring himself to laugh off their words.

He returned his attention to his work, pondering the things he had learned.

They worked in silence for a while.

"What did you mean last night?" Aric asked, suddenly starting up the conversation once more.

"Huh?"

"Last night. You were shouting about us not knowing what it meant."

"Oh." Olifur stared down at his feet. "I'm... I'm saving up my stin to help someone."

Aric nodded. "Sending it home to your family?"

"Something like that."

"A lot of us do that."

So not everyone here was an orphan. Olifur looked around at the grimy boys he had been working with for nearly a lunat and saw them with fresh eyes.

"Then they should understand," he muttered. "They shouldn't steal."

"When you're that desperate, what choice do you have?" Aric lifted a shoulder, unconcerned by the gravity of the deed.

Olifur scowled. "It's wrong."

"Maybe." Aric didn't sound convinced. "Maybe it's wrong to leave your money where people can easily take it."

Shaking his head, Olifur turned his attention back to his job, polishing the axles with more force than usual. He needed to make that money back, and fast. Fritjof's life depended on it.

12

DOJHUR

At the end of his last shift for the sennight, Olifur descended the stairs and collected his wages from Sooki, who always parted with the small sums reluctantly. He pocketed his coins and headed out the door, having determined that from now on he would stash his pay with his bow in the forest instead of inside his mattress. The coins that were meant for Fritjof would be far safer there. The other boys rarely left the Platte, and he had never encountered anyone inside the forest. Fritjof had always believed in letting the boys in his care learn things the hard way. This was just another hard-learned lesson that Olifur knew he would not soon forget. The two stin made a lonely sort of jingle in his pocket.

Once outside, standing on the street, he savored the precious freedom of an entire night and day to himself. A part of him longed to strike out for the forest and spend as much time as he could among the trees away from the crowds, but the thought of glimpsing the woman made his feet turn toward the inner circles of the city instead. Later, he would sleep in his tree and spend the morrow fishing, but tonight, he would carry out his accustomed vigil. It began to drizzle, but he had never known weather to deter her from keeping her appointments. Ducking his head, Olifur headed up the road toward the park.

He found her quickly this evening. There she was, strolling beneath the trees, her arm tucked into the tall man's elbow. Olifur trailed along after them for a while, hoping to catch a glimpse of her smile, but she wore a shawl around her head to keep off the rain.

Leaves were beginning to burst from the ends of branches here, livening up the dreary starkness of the park. Even in the dark, Olifur could now better imagine what it might look like with a canopy of green overhead and bright splashes of color in the flowerbeds below. Perhaps not all of Melar was ugly and dirty all the time. The woman paused to scatter some seeds, and small birds fluttered down behind her to peck at them and hop along the path.

Someone bumped into Olifur and he reflexively jerked away from the sudden contact with a loud huff of breath. His pocket tore, and the two small coins clinked against the gravel path. Olifur swooped down on them possessively, gripping them in his fist; panic at the thought of losing these, too, surging through him. He whirled about and stared up into the grinning face of a boy who looked to be slightly older than himself. Olifur narrowed his eyes and considered him. Several inches taller than himself, with a mop of dark hair escaping in wisps from beneath a low-slung cap, the boy's dirty face lit with an expression of mischief. His clothes were every bit as tattered as Olifur's own. His pants were baggy and too short, with much-patched knees. Over a ratty shirt he wore a too-big jacket that fell down past his knees, with the cuffs rolled up several times.

"Sorry, mate," the older boy said. "Didn't mean to rip your pocket."

"I'll bet," Olifur flashed, feeling the anger of the night before rising within him once more. "Just meant to pick it."

The older boy raised his hands and danced back a step, laughing. "Whoa! A guy's gotta eat. Can't blame me for trying."

Olifur glared at him. "You could try honest work."

The older boy shrugged. "Not as much fun."

Olifur turned his back dismissively, his gaze sweeping the park until he caught sight of the woman once again. He took a step in her direction, but found himself arrested as the other boy suddenly grabbed his arm, holding him in place.

"How come you're following Nneka?"

A shock coursed through him as the other boy suddenly entrusted him with this precious information. Her name! He had wondered what it might be—imagined hundreds of different names for her—once he had even attached his own dear mother's name to her, but he had dismissed that notion as a childish fancy almost immediately.

"Nneka?" he whispered to himself. Yes, the name fit her. It was lovely as she, and yet unassuming and modest like her, as well.

"Well?" The boy fixed him with a ferocious stare. "Why are you following her?"

Olifur's mind raced. "I wasn't following her," he protested, wincing as the lie left his lips. He had been following her, of course, but with no ill-intent.

"You were, so," the boy retorted. "I see you out here most every night, always trailing along after her. You fixing her as a mark of some kind? I wouldn't, iffen I were you. Sowke wouldn't like it. She's his, you know." The boy jerked his head toward the man escorting the woman, Nneka, along the pathway, getting farther and farther away with every step.

Olifur watched them go, lost in thought. He wondered if he would ever muster up the courage to speak to her. He wondered about the man, Sowke. Was he good to her? Surely someone so radiant would only be surrounded by people as kind and compassionate as herself. A warmth spread through his chest at the thought of the man, the one whose face he had never managed to see, Sowke. He must cherish her so, Olifur thought, remembering how they had walked along, arm in arm, so close together. Probably, he protected her fiercely from every sorrow that might cross her path. And though the man was not always with her, it must be nice for her to know that he was looking out for her. He was glad she had someone to take good care of her. A pang sliced through him; a longing for the kind of care he had once enjoyed from his parents, and from Fritjof. Being on his own was harder than he'd expected, and lonelier, too.

"Hey. You all right?"

Olifur blinked. "Yes."

"What's your name?"

"Olifur." His reaction came automatically, his brain still spinning as it tried to process what he had just learned.

"Name's Jens. But everyone calls me Dojhur." The boy stuck out his hand. "Pleased to meet you."

Olifur stared at the hand in a sort of dazed confusion. "What?"

"Pleased to meet you." Dojhur took Olifur's empty hand and clasped it. "Not many people can catch me trying to pick their pocket. It's an honor. Either you're quick, were already on your guard, or I'm getting sloppy."

"Pleased to meet you," Olifur repeated numbly.

Dojhur gave him an inquisitive look. "You ill?"

Olifur shook his head. How could he explain that a ready hand of friendship felt foreign here in this strange, cold city? How could he explain how lonely he had been? Or how homesick? A part of him desperately wanted to accept the hand of friendship that Dojhur seemed to extend, but a tight, bitter part of him eyed the other boy's cheerful grin and dancing eyes with a high degree of suspicion. His fingers tightened around his two stin protectively.

Dojhur wrapped an arm around Olifur's shoulders. "Come on, you look like you might need to sit a spell."

Olifur let the boy lead him down a dark alley and through a maze of twists and turns. Finally, Dojhur darted down a set of steps and Olifur suddenly stood inside a large, cave-like area in a cellar below a short building. He glanced around, taking in his surroundings. An oil lamp set on the table gave the room a warm glow. Large pieces of bright fabric unevenly stitched together partitioned the cellar into three rooms. Beyond one curtain, he could see several hammocks hanging from the ceiling in a myriad array of bright colors, and Olifur's heart ached at the familiar sight. An ancient and tiny wood-burning stove sat next to the foundation, its bent pipe stuck haphazardly through a broken cellar window to vent the smoke. Despite the musty smell and the dirt floor, the place had a cheery feel to it and Olifur found himself more comfortable here than anywhere else he had been inside Melar. The stove gave off a cozy heat that filled the small space.

Dojhur puttered around with a pot on the stove while Olifur sat on a low stool and gazed around, taking in his surroundings. The older boy finally finished and brought over two cracked mugs full of something that smelled like apples. He handed one to Olifur and sat down on another stool nearby. Olifur sipped cautiously at the steaming liquid and found it sweet and a little tart, but pleasant.

"What is it?" Olifur asked.

"Apple cider," Dojhur replied. "You've never had apple cider before?"

Olifur thought back as far as he could, but so much of his life before Fritjof's Glen was a blur in his memory. He had clear pictures in his mind of his parents and of small things like playing with his mother's locket, or riding on his father's shoulders, but little remained of the years before the bandits, before the forest. Many of the foods he had eaten, even the house he had lived in, picnics, special trips, learning to read... these were things he knew in his head that he had done and experienced—he had known how to read before he met Fritjof—but he had no recollection of them actually happening.

Shaking his head, he took another sip of the hot liquid, enjoying the way he could trace its warmth from his mouth as it trickled down his throat and then all the way to his stomach.

Dojhur eyed him. "So why *were* you following Nneka? And don't deny it. Like I said, I've seen you out before and you're almost always where you can see her. I'm just warning you because I sort of think I like you, Olifur: Nneka's not anybody's mark."

Olifur scrunched his face up at Dojhur in confusion. "Mark? I don't know what that means. I just..." He paused. How could he explain that she was like sunshine after a sennight of rain, or the stars shining down like dazzling bits of heaven on a clear night in the glen? How could he tell this stranger of the fierce, protective love he held for someone he had never spoken to? How could he explain that she drew him to her because she was the only thing in the entire wretched city that seemed pure and clean, the only person he had seen give away only kindness?

"She reminds me of my mum," Olifur finally whispered. It sounded feeble and not enough. But even as he spoke, he realized the truth of the words. From the first moment he had seen her, he had noted how similar she looked to his own dear mother, but he had never said the words out loud, never allowed himself to dwell on the way she reignited the ache in his heart at losing his own family.

Dojhur nodded, satisfied by the answer. "What happened to your parents, then?"

Olifur closed his eyes. Nobody had ever asked him that. Even Fritjof had kept quiet about the event, and he was the only one who had seen their graves. The older man had seemed to understand the private pain Olifur carried with him and had never pried into it. Perhaps, if he still lived, if Doctor Sveljen could help him, there would come a day when Olifur could speak to Fritjof about it, recounting the details of that terrible day. But he did not know if that time would ever come, now.

In a tidal wave of words, he poured the story out to this near stranger. He only kept the names of the two villains from passing through his lips. Something about saying their names out loud seemed somehow too dangerous, too difficult here in the dim glow of lamplight. Getting past the murder of his parents, Olifur then found himself telling Dojhur all about Fritjof and his glen and the other boys. Of everything that had transpired in the past three years. He told about his dangerous job at the Platte, his struggle to earn money for the doctor who had promised to help Fritjof, and how the other boys had robbed him. It felt good to tell his story, like setting down a weight he had been carrying far too long.

Dojhur listened carefully, not interrupting, until the story had finished. "You're lucky," he said at last. "At least you knew your parents."

Olifur frowned. "Didn't you?"

Dojhur shook his head, his expression melancholy. "Both died before I was born, I think."

Olifur nodded, then paused, tilting his head to one side as he pondered how such a thing might be possible. Before he could query further, however, Dojhur had risen to his feet.

"You want to meet Nneka?" he asked, his cheerful demeanor returning. "And the rest of my crew?"

"Your crew?" Olifur asked, startled out of his previous train of thought.

"Sure." Dojhur lifted his arms expansively. "You don't think I managed a grand hideout like this on my own?"

Olifur frowned. The thought hadn't occurred to him, partially because the cellar, while cozy, hadn't struck him as grand in any sense of the word. But he didn't comment, because the part of his brain that had been growing drowsy suddenly latched onto the other thing his new friend had said.

"You know Nneka?"

Dojhur grinned. "Of course. Why else would I care if you were following her?"

Olifur leaped to his feet. "I can meet her?"

"Sure."

"Right now?"

Dojhur laughed outright. "I can arrange that. Come on." He rose to his feet and ambled back outside. "This way."

Olifur scrambled after him, nearly falling on his face in his eagerness. Dojhur led them around the building and back into the park. Olifur blinked, surprised at how swiftly they had returned to where they had started from. So he had been correct earlier. Dojhur had been winding him around in circles, but they had not actually traveled far. The moon had risen while he and Dojhur had been talking. He scanned the area, searching for a familiar figure. He found her a moment later; Nneka was now bent over a small patch of earth on her hands and knees in a fenced-off corner of the park. The man was nowhere to be seen, and Olifur felt sorry. He would have liked to meet the man who loved Nneka and took care of her. It would have been nice to shake his hand.

"Community garden," Dojhur explained as they walked over. "Our crew has a small patch here. Ho, Nneka!"

The woman looked up and smiled brightly at them, pushing a strand of her pale hair away from her face with the back of her wrist. "Ho, Jens. Who's your friend?"

Dojhur put an arm around Olifur and pushed him forward. "This is Olifur. He's new to the city, and he's been working at the Platte."

Nneka smiled softly. "Welcome to Melar, Olifur."

Olifur stared at the woman, sudden shyness paralyzing his tongue. He cast his eyes to the ground, feeling his face grow uncomfortably warm. He blessed the dim light that hid his blush from her.

"Are they treating you well at the Platte?" she asked.

The genuine care and concern in her voice warmed him through, and he managed a single nod.

"Quiet one, isn't he?" Nneka commented.

"They've already robbed him once," Dojhur said. "And the food sounds horrible. And his bed is just moldy straw."

"Poor lad." Nneka brushed her hands together, dusting away

the dirt, and rose. "We can get him some better fare, can't we, Jens? Come along."

Olifur might not have moved had Dojhur not prodded him slightly in the back, propelling him forward. Silently, the two boys followed her around the corner and back into the cellar hideout, where Nneka began rustling around in cabinets, quickly throwing various items into the pot sitting on top of the stove.

"The others will be back soon," she said. "You just sit there and we'll introduce you when they get here."

Olifur sat on the stool, feeling bemused and enjoying the warmth and the pleasant smells that soon emanated from the pot. He still couldn't quite believe that any of this was truly happening. Slowly, other young boys trickled into the cellar and the rooms filled with laughter and joking and a general sort of boisterous camaraderie. Nneka greeted them each with a delighted smile and introduced Olifur, drawing him into the warmth of their circle and making him feel welcome and a part of this strange family. And yet it was not so strange. Although different from the glen, the rollicking and chatter was reminiscent of Fritjof's school, and soon Olifur felt right at home.

There were only five other boys besides himself and Dojhur, but in the small, enclosed space, it felt like more. Dojhur self-importantly gave the others a quick run-down of Olifur's story when they had all assembled at the table, and everyone eyed him sympathetically. They were all orphans, or runaways, it seemed. But none of them had ever been outside the city, and they were eager to hear about life in the glen. Olifur found himself the sudden center of much admiration when he told of making his own bow. And recounting life in the glen somehow earned him instant hero status.

"You live outside? No roof at all?" one boy asked with wide eyes. "And you hunt all your own food?"

The rest of them shook their heads, seeming impressed.

Two of the other boys had experience at the Platte, but neither of them had lasted longer than a sennight. They were telling him about their own time there, when the door suddenly opened once more and a much taller figure ducked through. It was the man, the one Olifur had often seen with Nneka, the one Dojhur had referred to as Sowke. His heart leaped at the chance to meet the man, to shake his hand, as he had hoped to do earlier. Olifur glanced up as the man slunk through the door, his thin frame hunched at the shoulders, his long coat whirling about his knees as he closed the door behind him. He swept off his tall hat and tossed it onto a hook, rubbing his hands together.

"Who's this, then?" The tall, thin man straightened and peered down at Olifur with dark, piercing eyes.

"Bale, this is Olifur," Nneka said, wiping her hands on her apron and going up on her tiptoes to give the man a quick kiss. "He's new to the city, and he works at the Platte."

"The Platte, eh?" Bale's eyes gleamed with sudden interest, but Olifur barely noticed. Horror coursed through him, freezing him in place.

That name! That face! That voice! A shudder rippled down his spine, sending his thoughts careening three years into the past. Once again, he was just a small boy cowering on the side of the dusty road. The bandits' leers pierced his memory, stabbing him through the heart. Dirt turning crimson. Sobbing. His own screams reverberating in his memory. The rocks were heavy, so very heavy. And his heart hurt so much. Everything hurt. Everything ached. Everything was darkness and despair. Olifur gasped for air, pulling the pieces of himself back together from where the winds had momentarily scattered them. He shook his head fiercely. It couldn't be the same man. He blinked and looked again, hoping he had been wrong. But no, he would never forget that narrow face, those cruel eyes. Bile rose in his throat and he choked, remembering how often he had seen Nneka clinging to the man's arm, the way she had embraced him just now. No. She would not be so friendly with someone like that. She would not... *could not* belong to the man who had murdered his parents.

13

DEN OF THIEVES

B ale Sowke sat down at the table across from Olifur and smiled. Olifur stared at the man's face, trying to block out the memories it had brought. Terror gripped its hands around his throat, slowly squeezing. He could not run screaming into the night. The man clearly did not recognize him, and why should he? Olifur had been nothing to him, just a cruel joke in the wake of his callous murder and theft.

"So, Olifur, is it?" Bale peered down at him. "Welcome to our humble home. How are they treating you over at the Platte?"

Olifur's heart spasmed. How could he sit here and speak casually with this monster? And yet how could he do anything else? If the man suspected for one second that Olifur had witnessed his crimes, he was certain the man would slit his throat without hesitation. And nobody in the room would stop him. Not even Nneka. Olifur let his gaze drift over to her for a single heartbeat in time, and he felt his heart close in on itself. How could she?

But he did not allow himself the luxury of any further thought. He looked up into Bale's dark eyes and shrugged. "I don't have any friends there, but they pay me at the end of every sennight."

Bale threw back his head and chortled. "Dojhur, where did you find this boy?"

Dojhur grinned. "Seen him around here and there a lot lately."

"And you are new to the city? Where did you live before?" Bale asked.

"In the forest," Olifur said.

"The forest?" Bale frowned at him, a mocking note entering his voice. "What did you do in the forest?"

"Hunted," Olifur replied.

Bale chuckled. "I see." He turned to Dojhur. "What did you bring him here for?"

"Thought he might be a good addition to the crew." Dojhur shrugged. "Thought I could offer him work that pays better than the Platte's two stin a sennight."

"Did you?" Bale narrowed his eyes. "Maybe so. Would you like that, lad? Being a part of our crew?"

Everything in Olifur screamed "No!" but he merely tilted his head and considered the man. "I don't know," he said. "Maybe. What kind of work do you do?"

"Hunting," Bale replied with a sly wink at Dojhur.

Nneka set a bowl of stew before Bale and gave him one of her brilliant smiles. He caught her by the wrist and pulled her into his lap with a grin. "What do you think of him, Nneka?"

The woman turned her smile on Olifur. "I think he's a dear."

She pecked Bale on the cheek with her lips and tried to rise, but he held her fast. "A dear, eh? But what do you think of him joining our crew?" he asked.

"Bale, I have to get everyone else their dinner," Nneka said. Her tone was laughing, but Olifur glimpsed a sudden shadow cross her eyes and he wondered what it meant.

"Answer my question first," Bale said. His lips curved upward, but his tone was hard.

Nneka stilled and gave Olifur a considering look. "I like the look of him," she said at length, her tone reluctant. "But it should be his decision."

"Of course," Bale said easily, finally releasing her. She slipped back to the pot and began spooning stew into more bowls.

Olifur's hands ached, and he looked down, surprised to find that he had been clenching them into fists below the table. He slowly uncurled them, his fingers resisting the change in position. Nneka set a bowl in front of him and she ruffled his hair playfully before returning to the stove.

"Want to join my crew?" Bale asked.

Olifur frowned and turned to Dojhur. "Thought you said it was your crew?"

Dojhur gave an uncomfortable little laugh as Bale turned a sudden, piercing gaze on him.

"Did you now?" Bale drawled.

"Just meant I wasn't on my own," Dojhur hedged. "Of course you're the leader, Bale."

Bale nodded, then turned his attention away from Dojhur and slurped up his stew in great spoonfuls. "Well, Olifur?"

Olifur shrugged. "Dunno." He had a feeling that turning Bale down flat would be a perilous move, but he had no intention of working with the murderer. Especially if his suspicions about Bale's particular brand of "hunting" were correct.

Bale smirked and fixed his gaze on Dojhur and the other boys. "Well, Dojhur, you've found us all a new friend. Do you have anything useful to show for your hunting today?"

Dojhur spread his arms and a variety of objects suddenly dangled from his hands and wrists. Chronometers backed in silver and gold, a rope of pearls, several silk scarves, and one large coin all appeared as if by magic. One by one, he set the items on the table in front of Bale. The man smiled appreciatively as he pocketed the coin and the rope of pearls.

"Very good," he said. Then his glance trailed around to the other boys. "And the rest of you?"

The others all clambered over one another in their haste to

produce their offerings. Soon, the table was piled high with various goods, from bolts of cloth to jewelry to an entire pie. Olifur stared at the growing mound, his worst suspicions confirmed. Hunting, indeed!

Bale winked at Olifur. "Do you like our quarry, lad? Think you could learn to stalk such prey?"

Olifur wanted to say something clever and witty, something casual and full of confidence, but all he could think of was how horribly vulnerable he had felt when he realized his pouch of coins had been taken. He understood that everything on the table had been stolen, but he also had a prickling sensation on the back of his neck that if he objected, he might be in danger. Visions of Bale's knife glinting in the sun filled his memory. So he merely shrugged and filled his mouth with a spoonful of stew, wondering how he could politely extricate himself from the situation and the cellar. He longed to escape. To race down the road out of Melar and into the forest. To run and run and never look back once until he was safely back in his own dear glen with Bet. Maybe Fritjof had gotten better on his own. Maybe he would return to find things as they had been before Fritjof got sick. Hope and despair warred together in his thoughts.

"Oh, stop teasing him, Bale." Nneka came to his rescue. She patted Olifur on the head again. Thunder rumbled outside and a pitter-patter of rain suddenly sounded on the ground outside the door. Nneka glanced out the window. "Olifur, would you like to spend the night with us? It's miserable out there. I hate to think of you having to walk back to the Platte in all that."

His heart ached at the kindness in her tone. How could someone like her live in this den of thieves? He almost shook his head, willing to sleep outside in a thunderstorm or even return to his uncomfortable pallet rather than spend the night under the same roof as Bale, but something stopped him and instead he gave her a tentative smile.

"I'd like that," he said.

Bale slapped one thigh. "You boys get off to bed. Find a hammock for Olifur, right? In fact, he can have Zek's old one."

The atmosphere in the cellar chilled as the chatter ceased and all the boys stared at the ground. The silence drew out, long and uncomfortable. Bale glowered at them. "What's wrong with you all?" he demanded, his lip curling into a feral sneer.

Dojhur cleared his throat, breaking the tense silence. "Come on, Olifur, I'll show you where you can bunk." He put an arm around Olifur and guided him through the curtain into the room with the hammocks. "You can sleep in this one," Dojhur said, indicating a blue hammock.

"Who's Zek?" Olifur asked in a hushed voice.

Dojhur's cheerful expression faltered briefly, then returned. "He used to be part of the crew."

"What happened to him?" Olifur asked. He suddenly felt that it was important to know.

Dojhur's mouth quirked to one side. "Caught by the guards," he said. "Hung."

Olifur stared, uncertain how to respond. "How old was he?"

"Maybe nine?" Dojhur shrugged. "Not sure. Most of us don't keep track of our ages, but Zek was one of the youngest."

Olifur's insides squirmed. On the one hand, justice had been served to a thief caught in the act. On the other hand, the severity of the punishment for a boy younger than himself horrified him.

Dojhur forced a grin. "If you can't bite, don't show your teeth, right?"

Olifur frowned, confused. "What does that mean?"

"It's nothing. Just a saying. One of Bale's sayings. It means..." Dojhur paused. "If you're stupid enough to make a mistake that gets you caught, then you deserve what you get."

"But Zek didn't make a mistake," one of the other boys suddenly said in a low tone. "He was just the lookout..."

"Shut your mouth, Mikko." Dojhur whirled on the other boy with frightening intensity, his expression dark with warning.

"But you said that Zek would have got away clean if he hadn't circled back to pull the guards off of Bale's scent..." Mikko protested.

"I didn't say it with Bale in the next room," Dojhur hissed. "Now shut your mouth and go to bed!"

Mikko, his eyes lighting with sudden fear, practically fled to the other side of the room, where he dove into his hammock and disappeared under a thick quilt. Olifur stared at Dojhur, pieces of the puzzle clicking into place.

Dojhur grimaced. "Maybe I shouldn't have brought you here," he muttered.

"Why did you bring me here?" Olifur asked, suddenly curious.

"I don't know," Dojhur said, staring at the ground as though unable to meet Olifur's eyes. "It was a bad idea."

Olifur frowned. "What was a bad idea?"

Dojhur suddenly met his gaze, his eyes dark and flashing with an emotion Olifur didn't recognize. "Nothing. I said it was a bad idea. In the morning, you go back to the Platte and just... stay there. It's safer for you there."

Mystified, Olifur climbed into the hammock. He settled into the familiar position and swung gently, staring up at the ceiling. The other boys were soon snoring, but Olifur found he couldn't sleep. He could hear Bale and Nneka's voices coming from where they still sat at the table, but he couldn't quite make out their words. His thoughts tumbled about as he pondered the events of the evening.

He must have drifted off for a bit, but a sudden thump pulled him back to wakefulness. Olifur lay in the hammock, his eyes adjusting slowly to the deep blackness. What had woken him?

"Bale, it's not a good idea." Nneka's voice reached his ears, and Olifur stilled, suddenly wide awake.

"But just think, Nneka," Bale said, his voice low and wheedling. "Just one cynder and we'd be set for life. With two or three, we could go anywhere in the world, see all those places you're always talking about."

"That would be lovely." Nneka's voice turned soft.

"You're a princess, Nneka. You should be treated like one."

Nneka said something too soft for Olifur to hear. For a moment, he strained his ears, trying to catch more of the words. Then Nneka spoke again, her voice full of worry. "It's too dangerous, Bale. If you got caught..."

"We could do even more." Bale's voice took on a hard edge. "With the right amount of power, we could topple the Ar'Mol himself."

"Bale!"

"Just think about it," Bale said. "I could set you up in the palace. You'd be a real princess, with every luxury you've ever wanted. You deserve it all, Nneka. Without you, where would I be?"

Nneka gave a forlorn little laugh. "It's just a dream. I don't need all that stuff, anyway."

"Yes, you do." Bale's voice turned hard and angry. "You deserve jewels and silks and a palace."

"I don't want to be a princess, Bale, really, I don't," Nneka protested.

"You don't know what you want," Bale scoffed, his tone impatient. "But I'll show you. I'll get it all for you."

"But Bale... the cynders..." Nneka's voice faltered. "They're dangerous."

"Don't tell me you believe that nonsense about them being magical," Bale sneered.

"N-nooo..." Nneka drew out her denial a bit too long. "But Bale, nobody knows how they work. They might as well be magic. And the stories of them exploding frighten me. We have a good life here, don't we?"

The man gave a harsh bark of a laugh. "Good life? Wallowing here in a filthy cellar, pretending to care about a handful of brats destined for the hangman's noose?"

"Bale!" Nneka's voice came out in a scared little gasp.

"I know, I know, you actually care for the little thieves. You're too softhearted, Nneka."

"I do care, Bale. And if you're honest with yourself, you do, too." Nneka's voice sounded choked, and there was a soft shushing sound.

"Sure, sure I do. Don't worry your pretty head about it another moment," Bale said, his voice soft. "I'll take care of every-thing. You know who takes care of you."

"You do take care of me," Nneka replied. "But it's not just the boys I worry for. Bale, I care about you, too. I don't want to see any of you behind bars, or worse."

"You're too good for me, Nneka. You know that. I don't deserve you." Bale spoke quietly. "But you don't have to worry about me. I promise."

"He's not on cynder-transfer, you know," Nneka said. "You can't use him."

"I can wait. Boy like that, he'll get there quick. I can tell just by looking at him. Thinks he's better than everyone, and the over-seers will buy it. And then I'll have my chance."

"Bale..." Nneka's protest was soft, just above a whisper.

"What?" Bale's tone turned sharp and angry.

"Nothing."

"That's right. You let me take care of things."

Olifur waited, wondering if they would continue the conver-sation, but the room fell silent. After a while, the outside door opened and closed and no more conversation drifted to his ears. With nothing left to listen to, he finally fell asleep.

In the morning, Olifur woke to the sizzle of bacon and eggs cooking over the stove and the hubbub of playful banter and shouting.

"Good morning, Olifur," Nneka greeted him as he cautiously came through the faded curtain wall and out into the main room. "We're just about to have breakfast. Grab yourself a plate."

No trace of her conversation with Bale the night before lingered about her, even though he peered at her closely. He did as he was told and joined the line of other boys while Nneka doled out eggs and bacon to each of them. Then he sat at the table, being companionably jostled on either side, and enjoyed the best meal he'd had since coming to Melar.

After the meal, he insisted Nneka let him clean up the dishes, and she accepted with a strangely stunned expression. Dojhur, not to be outdone by the newcomer, joined Olifur at the sink and dried each dish, barking at the other boys to help put everything away. Nneka sat at the table, her eyes wide. For a few minutes, she seemed to be at a loss. Finally, she pulled out a basket of sewing and began threading a needle.

"What will you do with your day off, Olifur?" Nneka asked, her needle flicking in and out around a patch she was attaching to a pair of trousers.

Olifur hesitated. "I usually go out into the forest," he finally admitted, not sure why he was suddenly reluctant to share this information.

Nneka sighed. "That sounds lovely. I often wish I could get outside the city more often."

"Why don't you?" Olifur asked. "The forest isn't far."

Nneka's eyes took on a faraway expression. "I might. Someday." Then she shook herself. "Here"—she thrust a paper-wrapped package into his hands—"I made you a sandwich for later."

He smiled up at her, warmed by her concern for him. "Thank you."

Her eyes crinkled at the corners. "No, Olifur. Thank you. You've reminded me that there is light in the world. Now get on off with you." She swatted at his shoulder. "Go to your forest. Enjoy your day off." She turned to the others. "And you'd best get to work. Bale won't be happy with a sparkling kitchen and no treasures."

He hesitated, loath to leave her presence. The other boys fairly scrambled over each other to get out the door, their boisterous shouts echoing down the alley. Olifur lingered, his gaze on the woman.

"Nneka..." he began, not even sure what he wanted to say to her.

She glanced up from her sewing and gave a small chuckle. "You still here? Go on, get!" A strange undercurrent of urgency pierced her words like a warning.

Dojhur, a small satchel slung over his shoulder, emerged from the back room and draped an arm around Olifur. "Come on, Olifur," he said. "Nneka wants us out from underfoot." He gave Nneka a quick nod, and something unspoken and fearful passed between them. Then Dojhur spun Olifur about and ushered him out through the door.

They had just made it around the corner when suddenly Bale loomed up over them, slinking out of the shadows like a nightmare. Olifur felt Dojhur's arm tighten around his shoulders and he suddenly got the idea that perhaps Dojhur felt a certain amount of unease in their leader's presence.

"Dojhur. Olifur." Bale nodded down at them. "Good hunting, lads."

Olifur stared up into the dark, soulless eyes and felt the same sort of creeping terror he had felt when the grymstalker had leaped out of the rocks and attacked Fritjof. Dojhur gave a noncommittal raise of one shoulder and directed Olifur in a sort of duck around the tall man. Olifur couldn't help but glance over his shoulder as they strolled down the street. Bale lurked just inside the shadow of the building, his eyes fixed on their retreating backs, two dark brands of fire piercing through them. Olifur averted his gaze and couldn't quite contain the violent shiver that coursed through him.

"Come on," Dojhur urged. "I want to show you something."

Olifur followed reluctantly. He desperately wanted to spend some time in the trees. He needed to get away from this den of thieves, to extricate himself from their company and never return. He could not take Bale up on his offer to join the crew, even if it meant earning money more swiftly. Fritjof would never approve of stealing, even to save his own life. Olifur also needed time to process all that had happened in the past day. Never once in the past three years had he imagined he would ever be face-to-face with his parents' murderer again. The encounter had shaken him, and he wasn't sure what to do about it. The guards wouldn't listen to a tattered boy, and besides, a murder committed three years ago miles away from the city's outskirts might not worry them overmuch.

He was following Dojhur, lost in his own thoughts, and trying to figure out a way to extricate himself from the company of his new acquaintance, when he turned a corner and found himself tumbling backwards from the sudden force of colliding with another person. Olifur flailed, trying to maintain his balance, but the force had been too great and he sat down hard on the muddy road.

"What do you think you're doing?" An angry voice reached his ears, but Olifur could not focus well. He rubbed his forehead where it had encountered the individual's waistcoat buttons and looked dazedly up into an angry round face staring down at him.

"Forgive me, sir," he stammered. "I wasn't paying attention."

"Watch where you're going next time," the man shouted at him. Then he stepped around Olifur and continued on his way.

"Nice job."

Olifur blinked and looked up to see Dojhur hanging out a window above him.

"How did you get up there so fast?" Olifur asked.

"I'll show you. Get moving," Dojhur hissed.

Olifur rubbed his head again and climbed to his feet when a shout and a sudden clamor behind him made him pause and turn.

"Get up!" Dojhur hissed. "You need to get out of here!"

"Wha—"

"Thief!"

The shout reverberated around the street, paralyzing Olifur in his place. Involuntarily, he glanced up at the window, but Dojhur had disappeared inside. Before he could even feel any guilty relief that his friend had gotten away, Olifur felt himself being yanked around by his collar. He choked a bit as his shirt bit into his neck, and swung around to see the man who had bumped into him looming over him once more.

"Where are my coins, you little thief?" the man bellowed down at him. "Send for the guards! Someone fetch a guard!"

"Sir!" Olifur choked. "I didn't..."

The man shook him, screaming incoherently into his face, and Olifur found he couldn't get a word in through the noise and his shirt collar slowly strangling him. A crowd gathered around them in a circle, and other voices joined the man's, bemoaning the abundance of pickpockets and thieves in their beautiful city. The man punctuated every shouted phrase by shaking Olifur roughly.

Then the crowd parted as a stocky man burst through the circle.

"What's this?"

Olifur glanced up in relief at the familiar voice as Garth's face came into view. The guard stared down at him through narrowed eyes, but gave no indication he had recognized Olifur.

"This young pickpocket pilfered my purse a moment ago when he bumped into me coming round this corner," the man said, his volume slightly lower now, but no less angry.

"Is that so?"

"I know their tricks," the man replied proudly. "That's why I checked my pockets afterwards."

"I see." Garth rubbed his chin. "And have you found your purse now that you have apprehended the guilty party?"

The man faltered. "I have not had the chance to search him yet, Lieutenant. I wanted a guard present as witness."

"Very well." Garth knelt down before Olifur and swept his hands up and down the boy and then made him show his open hands. Olifur stared at him, silently begging him to understand that he had been wrongly accused, but Garth still did not look into his eyes. After a moment, the guard stood. "This boy has no purse on him. Just two stin in one pocket. Are these yours?"

The man hesitated briefly, a greedy gleam in his eye. "They might be. How am I to know what he removed from my purse until I find it and check the entirety of its contents?" He swooped down on the coins, but Garth closed his hand over them.

Garth shook his head. "And where do you think he may have put your purse? Did he have time to dart off somewhere or throw the purse into a hiding spot?" The guard peered around at the onlookers who had gathered. "Did any of you see what happened?"

One little old lady came forward with slow, hobbling steps. "Sir, I did not see the whole of it, but I did see that man come around the corner and knock the boy down." Her quavering voice rose, and she glared around at the crowd. "I felt sorry for the lad and was trying to get over to help him up when this man returned and lifted the boy from the street and started accusing him of theft. The child had no time to hide anything."

"Then he was still sitting in the street when this gentleman realized his purse was missing and came back?" Garth asked.

"Yes," the woman confirmed.

"I don't see how this boy could have stolen your purse," Garth said, his voice calm.

"He did it, I say!" the man insisted. "I say he needs to be locked up until he confesses and returns my purse."

"Lad." Garth spoke directly to Olifur now, looking him in the eye for the first time. "Did you take this man's purse?"

"No," Olifur said, his voice bitter. "He ran into me and knocked me over, and now he's aiming to steal my only two stin, earned fairly from the Platte where I work."

The man reared back, his face darkening as Olifur spoke in his clear, steady voice. "How dare he! Officer, I demand that you lock him up for impudence and insulting his betters. He stole my purse and now he accuses me of theft? The audacity! Young man, do you have any idea who I am?"

"You are a lout with no manners," Olifur replied steadily.

He never saw the blow coming. One moment he was standing in the street defiantly defending himself, and the next his ears were ringing as his world exploded in painful lights. He felt his head hit the ground and then darkness overtook him.

14

AFTERMATH

Olifur opened his eyes in a pale gray light. His head throbbed and his stomach ached. He lay on a narrow cot raised up off the floor and topped with a thin mattress. Memory emerged slowly, and Olifur sat up with a gasp, frantically digging his hand into his single pocket. His fingers touched the two small coins, and he heaved a sigh of relief; he did not know if he could bear being robbed a second time of his precious earnings.

"You're awake."

Olifur swung his head toward the voice and then winced as a wave of nausea overwhelmed him. He stared through metal bars at Garth, who sat in a chair at a desk on the other side of the bars. Rising, Olifur cautiously made his way over to the door of the cell in which he now resided. His stomach erupted with butterflies as he realized he was in a cage.

Garth waved a hand. "It's not locked. You're not a prisoner. But I needed somewhere safe to bring you, and this was the best I could do on short notice. I can't tell you how glad I am to see you standing up."

Olifur pushed experimentally on the door. It swung open. His stomach still fluttered about nervously, but it quieted as he stepped out of the cell and stood before the guardsman.

"How's your head?" Garth asked.

Olifur winced and reached up to feel the tender lump that had formed on the back of his head. "Sore."

"Sorry about that. I tried to stop him."

Panic snaked through Olifur and he leaped toward the window to peer out. "How long was I asleep? I have to get back to the Platte before dawn..."

"Slow down." Garth put out a hand. "You were only out for a little while. There's still a lot of daylight left if you're feeling well enough to enjoy it. But I hoped you might be willing to help me before you leave."

"Help you?" Olifur stared at the man. "With what?"

"Just answering a question or two," Garth said. "I know you didn't steal that man's purse. And after some arguing and searching of all the nooks and crannies around that corner, he admitted that you probably didn't do it, either. But I wondered if maybe you saw who did?"

Olifur stared at Garth. He had not seen anyone steal the loud man's purse. He certainly had a suspicion about who had done it, but he wasn't sure. To point a finger when he wasn't sure felt as wrong as doing the stealing himself. Shaking his head slowly, Olifur frowned. "I didn't see it happen."

"I thought not," Garth said. "It's even possible that someone snatched his purse before he even got to that corner and you became an easy suspect." The guard shrugged. "Or he'll get home and find he left it in a different coat. Anyway, you're free to go if you're feeling up to it."

Olifur smiled his thanks and opened the door out onto the street.

"One more thing." Garth's voice stopped him before he could step outside. "That older woman who spoke up for you said that you were walking with another boy, about your age, but that he disappeared just before things got interesting."

Olifur nodded. "Jens," he said. "I'm not sure where he ended up."

"New friend?" Garth asked.

"I'm not sure if he's a friend," Olifur replied truthfully.

He contemplated the guard sitting before him. Here was a man who might care about a young couple being murdered, even if it had happened ages ago. Garth was a good man, of that he was certain. Perhaps he could tell Garth about Bale. Garth was a guard. It would be his job to investigate. And yet Olifur hesitated. He had no proof. Just his own word about a memory from years in the past. Would Garth even believe him? Olifur wasn't sure. And he didn't know if he could bear being doubted again. He had seen the flicker of distrust in Garth's eyes before he had determined that Olifur did not have the belligerent fellow's purse. And besides, he did not wish to hurt Dojhur or Nneka if he could help it. No, there might be a time when he would confide in Garth, but that time was not now. Not yet.

Garth eyed him. "Well, it's good to be careful with strangers, even if they seem friendly."

"Words of truth."

"I'll see you around, Olifur. Make sure you watch out when going around corners." Garth's lips twitched slightly.

Olifur chuckled. "I will." He turned, and then paused, looking back at the guard. "Thank you, Garth."

It seemed too little, too small a thing, to simply say "thank you." But it was all he had to show his appreciation for the way the man had protected him. Garth glanced up and gave a gentle nod.

"Go on," the man said, waving him away.

Olifur stepped outside. The door swung shut behind him, and Olifur peered around, trying to get his bearings. In a few minutes, he realized he was near the west gate. The sun stood about halfway between the top of the sky and the horizon, indicating that Garth had spoken the truth: he still had plenty of daylight left. With long strides, Olifur made his way down the road leading out of the city. It was only a couple of miles to the edge of the forest, and by the time he reached the trees, the exercise had helped to clear his head a little. He breathed in the deep, earthy smell of the wood and the surrounding dirt, just taking it in and basking in the emerald glow of the great wood that began here and stretched south and west, away from the city. This was where he belonged.

He wended his way through the trees until he found the little rocky outcropping where he kept his bow, arrows, and knife. Unwrapping his bow and quiver, he used the knife to cut away a square of the canvas, into which he deposited his two precious coins. He tied the canvas into a little pouch, then dug into the soft earth beneath the outcropping until he had a shallow hole into which he placed the pouch, covering it quickly. He had learned his lesson: keeping his valuables within easy reach was a good way to lose them.

Shouldering his quiver, Olifur tramped through the forest in search of game. It took an hour, but eventually he brought down a widgeon shortly before sunset. He brought it back to his camp, which he had slowly been building over his off-days. It wasn't anything much: just a basic structure of sticks woven with leaves and thatch, not completely waterproof, but it kept most of the weather out. Inside, he had a soft bed of pine needles, which he enjoyed as a luxury once a sennight. Outside his hut he had built a fire ring, where he now spitted the duck. While he waited for the meat to turn a golden brown, he foraged nearby for wild onions and raspberries, which he found in greater abundance than before, now that spring had fully arrived.

When the duck had finished roasting, Olifur enjoyed a leisurely dinner and the warmth of the fire. Night had fallen, and high above, peeking through the leaves, the stars shone down, their faint light a strangely cold comfort. The stars never changed.

His thoughts drifted to Nneka and Dojhur and the other boys. He should avoid them, he knew. They were thieves, and he wanted nothing to do with theft. Fritjof had pounded honesty and respect for the possessions of others into his heart, and even if he had not, losing his parents to bandits would have impressed the lesson deeply into Olifur's soul.

And yet he had enjoyed their company. They had treated him kindly, shared their food and their roof with him. In spite of himself and their association with Bale, Olifur found that he cared about what happened to Nneka and Dojhur. He wanted to help them. But he wasn't sure they wanted help. Perhaps they saw nothing wrong with their actions. Perhaps they were all just as bad as the murderous Bale. He did not want to believe that of Nneka, or of the cheerful Dojhur, but that they remained with the man was concerning. The fact that they stole and cared so little about their targets gnawed at his thoughts. Questions plagued his soul. How could two people so kind and cheerful spend their days robbing others? How could they not see Bale for what he was? How could they live so closely with a murderer? Were they ignorant of his true nature? Or—he shuddered at the thought—complicit with it?

His thoughts tumbled against themselves for long hours until his fire burned down to embers. Finally, with a deep sigh, Olifur threw dirt onto the fire and stamped it out. Then he turned his face back east and tramped up the road to Melar and the Platte. He had no interest in being late for work in the morning and giving Hughin an excuse to thump him on the head with his cane.

———

OLIFUR AWOKE to discover that tragedy had struck in his absence. Aric informed him grimly that the cynder-loading had gone terribly awry the day before. A boy had tripped on his way to get another load of cynders, slipped through the tracks, and fallen to his death.

"Thankfully, they didn't drop the cynders," Aric said.

Olifur frowned at the callous remark. "A boy died," he said, aghast at how casually Aric could respond to the tragedy.

"And if a cynder had fallen from that height, what do you

think would have happened to the Platte?" Aric asked. "It's not just a rumor that the cynders explode if you hit them hard enough. It could have brought down the building and everyone inside it would have died. You would have come back to a pile of rubble. I'm sorry Geoff is gone, but I'm glad I'm still here."

Olifur nodded soberly, rattled by the idea of what might have happened. He had understood that the job was dangerous, but it startled him to find that after more than a lunat of swinging around under the trains and dabbing grease onto the axles and wheel hubs, he had also grown comfortable with the danger. It lived with him so closely, his constant companion, that he no longer felt wary of it. Even in the light of the recent tragedy, he could not dwell too long on the danger of his job as Hughin ordered them all to get to work. The motion of his job was an easy rhythm that he fell into and soon he was whistling as he darted about the great wheels, heedless of the vast distance between himself and the ground. Dodging death, cheating tragedy with every step he took, there was a certain thrill to it, he supposed, and a satisfaction he took in doing a job well, even if it was dirty and tedious and paid next to nothing.

"Olifur!"

The shout barely startled him as he finished the last wheel. Olifur stepped up onto the solid platform and looked up at the man towering over him. He tried not to cringe, but experience taught him that having Hughin's attention usually resulted in pain.

"Yes, sir?"

"With Geoff gone, we're short a loader. You're on that duty starting tomorrow," Hughin barked gruffly.

"Really?" Olifur stammered. "Why me? Aric is most senior."

"Seniority has nothing to do with it. Can't be a loader without steady hands, and yours are solid. More than any of the others on your team."

Olifur blinked. Had that been a compliment? Maybe, but it probably hadn't been given on purpose.

"So even though you're scrawny and undersized and new, you get the job. And an extra stin every sennight. Report to Sven on the ground level at dawn; he'll show you how to do your job." Hughin scowled down at him, his eyes narrowing as though he would like to have an excuse to rap him on the head with his cane.

"Thank you, Hughin."

Hughin stared at him for a long moment, as though trying to gauge whether Olifur's words were sincere. After a moment, he grunted and stomped away.

When he had finished his unappetizing dinner, Olifur turned in early. He told himself it was because he did not wish to jeopardize his new position by sleeping past dawn, but deep down, he knew he was avoiding Nneka and Dojhur. On his mattress, he tossed and turned, struggling to fall asleep at such an unaccustomed hour. The other boys eventually joined him, and he finally drifted off to sleep, lulled by the deep sounds of their breathing.

The next morning, he joined the other loaders, got his instructions from Sven, and the long day of back-breaking work began. First, they had to remove the depleted cynders from the engine of the train. These were loaded up into crates and carried downstairs, where they would be disposed of or shipped back to the refinery. Olifur didn't quite follow what happened to them once they were out of his care. The boys stacked the empty cynders behind the shed in an alleyway, where a cart would pick them up in the evening. Then, each of the three boys on the loading team had to transfer six cynders from the storage shed at the corner of the property up the seven flights of stairs where they loaded the full cynders onto the train. These had to be carried up one at a time, and they had to walk the steps slowly and carefully, so as not to jostle the cynders, trip, or risk dropping them. Once on the train, the cynders had to be inserted into their slots in the engine so that the train could depart. When they had finished this chore, the boys spent their remaining daylight hours polishing the interior of the train until every bit of it gleamed before it departed the station.

They had to do this three times throughout the day for the three different trains that arrived at the Platte Docking Station, each at a different time. Olifur's legs ached from all the traveling up and down stairs, and his arms often felt as though they were moving in circles of their own volition from the polishing motions.

Olifur wondered what it would be like to travel along the rails, gliding so fast and high above the ground, seeing places he'd only ever heard of, seeing places he'd never heard of. In between trips up and down the stairs, he let his mind wander slightly, though he kept his thoughts firmly on the task at hand whenever he was transporting a crate. Even the depleted cynders could still be dangerous, the other boys warned him. Sometimes they weren't completely empty, but they had to take them off the train and exchange them anyway.

As the day came to a close, Olifur wiped his forehead and breathed a deep sigh. When Sven had described the job to him, it hadn't sounded like much. But it had been a long day. And the stress of the work had frazzled his nerves to the core. He fell into bed, too exhausted even to pause for dinner.

The rest of the sennight proceeded in similar fashion, though Olifur soon found that skipping meals was a bad idea with his new position. As unappetizing as the offerings of the mess were, he needed the energy it gave him to do his work. The second day found him getting rapped sharply by Hughin's cane on every trip back and forth as he lagged behind the other boys.

By the end of the sennight, Olifur was exhausted to the depths of his soul. The extra stin did nothing to cheer him. He merely accepted it silently and made his way down the road to his forest hideaway, where he buried his new coins. The small stash of coins depressed him and caused his thoughts to tumble about in a worried cyclone. What if Fritjof grew so ill the doctor could not help him? Worse, what if he had already died and Olifur had missed his chance to say goodbye? Despite his worries, when he threw himself onto his bed of pine needles, his exhaustion overwhelmed him and he slept until well into the day. He only woke because of his complaining stomach. He had little luck with hunting, however. His hunger made him impatient and reckless, and he missed his mark several times. Finally, he tried his hand at fishing in the little stream and caught a couple of fish, which he cooked and ate with ravenous appetite.

The next morning, back at the Platte, the cycle began all over again, but Olifur found his muscles were growing accustomed to the new work. It was still mind-numbing and terrifying and difficult, but when he reached the end of the day, he found he still had a little energy left. His head and shoulders ached from the bruises left by Hughin's cane, but there were fewer of them than there had been a few days ago. He was getting faster and stronger. But the ordeal wearied more than his body. His soul longed to get away. He desperately needed to escape the Platte, to find a change of scenery. The few hours he had spent in the woods were not enough, especially since he had spent most of them sleeping.

Though he was reluctant to go back out into the city, Olifur told himself that he did not need to go to the places Nneka usually haunted. He could avoid Bale's crew. And he could sweep out Hildy's and get something to erase the taste of the Platte's latest supper from his tongue. Even Epps's stale biscuits were better than the Platte fare.

Shoving his hands deep in his pockets, Olifur headed towards Hildy's. He did not expect the warm welcome that awaited him. Master Epps's face brightened when he saw Olifur at the door.

"Young Olifur! I missed you the past several nights," the man said. "I worried you'd taken sick."

"I'm sorry I didn't come," Olifur said. "Work at the Platte has been difficult."

"I'm glad to see you," Epps said. He handed him a broom and Olifur took extra care sweeping up the shop. When he finished, Epps handed him a bulky bundle wrapped in paper. "I packed up a few of your favorites." He gave Olifur a friendly wink. "I realized

I might have been taking your hard work for granted a bit. I hope this makes up for it, at least in part."

Mystified, Olifur peeled back the corner of the package and found a small loaf of cardamom cake sprinkled with large granules of white sugar, two small saffron buns, and an entire baker's dozen of spice cookies. Nestled at the bottom of the package were two rectangular copper coins with the customary rod and scepter stamped on them: stin. His eyes widened at this bounty and he stared up at the baker.

Master Epps's eyes crinkled at the corners. "It's less than you deserve, lad. You've been a faithful help to me, easing my aching back in the evenings. When I mentioned that you hadn't been around lately, Hildy scolded me fiercely for my treatment of you. Those are all fresh, well, fresh today, anyway. I wasn't sure you'd be back, but I hoped. And I hope you'll come back tomorrow evening as well. I can't pay you much, but I can put a stin in your pocket every sennight if it helps. And no more stale biscuits. I promise."

A lump formed in Olifur's throat. "Thank you, Master Epps," he finally choked out. "I'll be back tomorrow."

Cradling the precious bundle of treats close to his chest, Olifur headed back out into the darkened city.

15

THE OFFER

A s he left Hildy's, Olifur had a vague idea that it would be pleasant to find Garth and share his unexpected largess, but although he saw plenty of other officers making their rounds, he did not spot his friend. Munching on a pepperkakor, he savored the crisp chewiness of the cookie between his teeth and the sharp flavors that danced across his tongue in a pleasant mixture of sweet and spicy. Aromas of cinnamon, cardamom, cloves, and a hint of ginger filled his nostrils, and he smiled as he ate, ancient memories of his mother's baking resurrected, filling his mind with comforts he thought he had forgotten. The cookies made him think of special celebrations and warmth and the feeling of being loved and cared for.

"Olifur!"

The familiar voice arrested him in his tracks and pulled him abruptly out of his pleasant thoughts. He turned as Dojhur trotted up behind him.

"Olifur!" Dojhur shook his head with a wide grin. "You're all right! You're free! I saw you get hit, and then that guard picked you up and carried you off. I thought they locked you up for sure!"

"Garth knew I hadn't done anything wrong," Olifur said,

trying to keep the reproachful tone out of his voice. "He took me to the gaol to keep me safe from that other man."

"Garth, eh?" Dojhur eyed him suspiciously. "You say that guard's name like he's a friend."

"He is." Olifur held out a cookie. "Pepperkakor?"

Dojhur accepted the treat and took a bite. He raised his eyebrows appreciatively. "Nice," he mumbled around the mouthful of cookie. "Where'd you lift this from? Tastes fresh."

Olifur frowned, confused at the unfamiliar term. "Lift?"

"You know, where'd you swipe it from?"

"I didn't steal it," Olifur replied stiffly. "I earned it."

"Sure, don't we all?" Dojhur winked at him.

Olifur gave a huff of exasperation. "I sweep out a shop up the way every night," he explained. "The owner pays me in day-old pastries. Tonight he gave me nicer ones as a gift. That's all."

Dojhur squinted at him. "You mean it."

"Course I do. Stealing is wrong."

"Ah." Dojhur gave him a look. "Er. Right." He frowned. "So when you say that you're friends with a guard... you actually mean it?"

"Sure. Why not?" Olifur replied.

"Huh. Well, I'm glad you're not locked up."

"Did you take that man's purse?" Olifur asked.

Dojhur blinked. "What?"

"The man who hit me," Olifur said, speaking with slow determination. "The one who accused me of stealing. Did you take his purse? You bumped into him when he ran into me. Bumped into him just like you did to me the first time we met and your hand ended up in my pocket. Did you take his purse?"

Dojhur put up his hands. "Whoa. Slow down there. Surely you don't think that I would have..."

"Did you?" Olifur demanded, unwilling to back down, unwilling to let the matter drop. "He accused me of stealing and I almost ended up locked in the gaol over something I didn't do. I think you owe me the truth."

Dojhur eyed him, then huffed out an exasperated breath. "I didn't mean for you to get in trouble over it," he muttered, a genuine note of regret in his tone. "If I thought for one second you'd just stand there like a loon, I wouldn't have let you. I did tell you to run."

"If you hadn't stolen, I wouldn't have had to run."

"Look..." Dojhur raised his hands in a helpless gesture. "If I don't bring stuff back to the cellar, Bale will make sure I disappear. It's not just that I can't go back. I'll turn up in a ditch with me throat cut."

Olifur's eyes widened. "Why do you stay, then?"

Dojhur sighed and kicked at the dirt. "Bale's taught me everything I know. It's the only thing I know. I don't like it, but I owe him. Without him, I'd be dead already, probably starved to death in the gutter somewhere. He took me in when no one else would."

"But you're scared of him," Olifur protested. "You all are. I saw the way everyone went pale when he mentioned Zek. And Mikko said..."

"Mikko should keep his mouth shut or he'll end up just like Zek," Dojhur whispered fiercely, his fists clenching. "And you shouldn't go talking about things you know nothing about."

Olifur gave the other boy a good, hard stare. Anger rose up inside him, but he merely pressed his lips together and swung around, heading back to the Platte. He walked quickly, taking long strides that carried him down the road swiftly.

"Wait! Olifur!"

Olifur refused to turn around or stop.

"Look... Olifur! Will you wait?"

He didn't falter or hesitate. Just kept walking.

Dojhur appeared at his elbow, panting a little as he trotted along. "Olifur." When Olifur didn't slow, Dojhur reached out and grabbed at the arm holding the small sack of pastries. Olifur twisted away and delivered a hard punch to Dojhur's stomach with his free hand. The older boy doubled over with a cough and Olifur turned away.

"Look, I'm sorry I got you in trouble," Dojhur wheezed out.

Olifur paused. He hadn't quite been expecting an apology. He didn't think "apology" was any part of Dojhur's vocabulary. Curious, he turned back around.

"What?"

"I'm sorry. Are you happy?" Dojhur straightened with a visible wince. "You're pretty strong, you know."

Olifur shrugged. "I carry heavy cynders up and down stairs all day, now. Those things are made out of rock, and they're big!"

Dojhur's expression fell slightly. "So they've moved you to loading duty, have they?"

"Yes." Olifur yawned. "It's getting late. I should get back."

"Olifur," Dojhur said, then hesitated. His face contorted strangely, and he seemed to be wrestling with something.

"Yeah?"

"Nothing." Dojhur gave him a soft punch to the shoulder, near a more recent bruise, and Olifur winced. "It's just good to see you're not locked up."

Olifur grimaced. He wanted to say something like "no thanks to you," but he sensed Dojhur had truly been sorry, and he didn't feel like starting that fight up again. Instead, he gave a jaunty little jerk of his head and smirked.

"Come by the cellar sometime," Dojhur said as Olifur started walking once more. "When I told Nneka what happened, she was worried about you. She'll be happy to know you're well."

Olifur felt a pang in his chest at the thought of Nneka being fearful for him, but he had no wish to enter the same space as Bale Sowke ever again. He dug out a handful of the pepperkakor and offered them to Dojhur.

"Take these to Nneka and the other boys for me?" he asked.

Dojhur stared down at the cookies, then looked up at Olifur. "You said these were a gift," he protested.

"Which means I can do what I want with them. And I want to give them to you and Nneka."

Dojhur accepted the cookies and pulled out a clean handkerchief in which he wrapped the treats almost reverently. "I'll carry them carefully so they don't break."

Olifur gave him a quizzical smile, uncertain about why Dojhur was acting so strange about the gift, but he shrugged. "I'm sure you'll get them safely back to the cellar."

Dojhur nodded studiously, his eyes fixed on the small package. He waved a vague farewell, and they parted ways.

———

It was several more sennights before Olifur saw Dojhur again. Although he kept his promise to Master Epps and returned every evening to sweep out Hildy's, often that was all the extra energy he could muster. He no longer wandered the streets after dark. Hughin had added cleaning the supply closet to Olifur's daily duties, and the additional chore wore him down and left him with little desire to go for long walks or do much of anything other than sleep. And he had no wish to meet up with Bale in the darkened streets or some shadowy corner. He couldn't trust himself not to confront the man with his own past, and he knew he couldn't win a fight against him. It would be safer to simply avoid him.

Master Epps was as good as his word, always saving a portion of his best treats for Olifur, a kindness that the boy looked forward to all throughout the day, and the baker often slipped an extra stin into Olifur's pocket as additional payment. In this way, his tiny store of coins grew more quickly than before, and he now had fifteen stin hidden away. Soon, he promised himself, he would have enough to pay the physician to come help Fritjof, and then he would leave the city for good, return to the glen, and never set foot in Melar again.

When he did see Dojhur again, the events that had led to his waking up behind bars had softened in his memory—after all, the door had not been locked and he had not ended up in any trouble. So he greeted Dojhur with a smile and agreed to come and see Nneka on the condition that he had no interest in seeing Bale. Dojhur didn't even blink at this condition, just nodded amiably before informing Olifur that the man had gone away on a long job with some of his older crew and wouldn't be back for a few days.

Nneka embraced Olifur, nearly weeping in her joy at seeing him safe and well with her own eyes. He shared out his pastries with her and Dojhur and they walked in the little park and talked. Nneka peppered him with questions about his life in the glen. She was interested in everything he had done there and expressed amazement at his knowledge of gardening. She led him over to her little plot of ground where she tended her vegetables and asked him questions, which he answered thoughtfully, showing her a few things that might help the plants grow better. He also taught her a few tricks she did not know about keeping the wildlife away from the tender plants.

A brisk wind kicked up and a light drizzle fell, chasing them inside the cellar, where Nneka put on a pot of hot water and brewed a weak tea.

Dojhur wanted to know about his hunting trips, and when Olifur recounted his one big hunt with Fritjof, the older boy seemed properly impressed.

"You fought off a grymstalker? For real?"

Olifur grinned and shrugged. "Mostly Bet fought it off. And Fritjof killed it with his arrow. I sort of just stood there being terrified."

Dojhur whistled. "I would have been, too. I can't believe you have a malkyn as a pet. I've always wanted to ride one."

"I got to ride one, once," Nneka said, setting two cups in front of them before retrieving her own and joining them at the table.

"When?" Dojhur demanded.

"Oh, so many years ago." Nneka waved a hand and sipped slowly at the tea. "I was very small. It was before my parents died." She smiled softly. "It is one of my fondest memories, though. It's hazy, but I remember that the creature's fur was softer than anything I'd ever felt before." She paused, considering. "Softer than anything I ever felt after, too."

Dojhur stared at her in admiration. Then his attention turned to Olifur's description of his bow. He wanted a complete explanation of how to make his own. He asked a thousand questions about the process and then asked if Olifur might teach him how to hunt and fish.

"It takes a long time to make a proper bow," Olifur warned him. "I don't have any staves seasoned—Fritjof always had several branches going at once—but I can teach you how to use my bow if you come out to the forest with me sometime."

"The forest?" Dojhur frowned. "What forest?"

Olifur squinted at his friend. "The one a few miles outside the city gates. I have a little camp out there. It's where I keep my bow, since it doesn't do me much good in Melar. I always stay out there on my day off."

Dojhur stared at him. "You mean you sleep outside? Every sennight? On purpose?"

Olifur grinned. "It's great. I built a little shelter, and my bed out there is softer than the one at the Platte. I look forward to it. The sounds of the forest are even better than my memories of my mum's lullabies when I was little."

Dojhur gazed off into the distance, his expression turning wistful. "With skills like that, you don't need to stay in Melar." He sounded envious.

"I don't plan to." The words burst out of Olifur before he had a chance to think about them, or to ponder the wisdom of sharing his deepest, most treasured dreams.

"What do you mean?" Nneka asked.

"I'm only in Melar to earn money for a physician," Olifur explained. "Fritjof is sick." He paused. "Really sick. He needs a good doctor, and there's one here in Melar. He promised to come help Fritjof if I can pay for his travel and the medicine Fritjof needs. I had hoped to be back in Elbian already, but"—he grimaced—"one of the other boys at the Platte stole my first lunat's wages. I had to start over."

Nneka gave him a sympathetic look.

"When do you think you'll have enough?" Dojhur asked.

"Maybe another sennight or two," Olifur said. "Sooner if I can get more paying jobs, like the one from Master Epps."

"And then you'll leave Melar?" Nneka's voice sounded wistful.

Olifur nodded. Then a thought struck him. "You could come with me."

Nneka gave a low gasp and began shaking her head in a quick denial.

But Dojhur pursed his lips. "Would you really let us tag along?"

"Of course," Olifur said. "The glen has plenty of space. And there's a cabin. Well, it needs a new roof, but we can fix it."

"I... I couldn't," Nneka whispered. "I couldn't leave Bale. Jens"—she turned to Dojhur, her eyes pleading—"you... you wouldn't..."

Olifur frowned at her. "Why not?" he burst out.

Nneka shook her head. "Bale took me in. Gave me a home. I had nothing before he found me. He takes care of me." She gazed at him, a liquid pleading in her eyes. "I... I love him, Olifur. And he loves me. He takes care of me. I can't make it on my own without him."

Olifur bit his lip. He did understand. Fritjof had done the same for him. He would have done anything for the old man. But Fritjof had never asked him to lie, or to steal. Had never asked him to look the other way while he hurt people. Had never spoken so casually about his lack of care for others the way that Olifur had overheard Bale doing the night he had stayed in the cellar. He wondered what Nneka would say if he told her that Bale had murdered his parents. She probably wouldn't believe him. The accusation wouldn't hurt Bale, but it would hurt Nneka, and Olifur had no wish to do that. He kept his tongue clenched between his teeth, resisting the urge to tell her exactly how much of a monster the man was.

"Besides," Nneka continued, her shoulders slumping, "he needs me. I couldn't just go off and leave him alone." She turned to Dojhur. "I can't make the decision for you, Jens. If you want to go..."

Dojhur's expression had gone suddenly blank and inscrutable. "No," he sighed. "You're right. It wouldn't work. He'd never let either of us go, anyway."

"Jens," Nneka protested. "Bale wouldn't hold you back from something you wanted."

Dojhur gave a harsh little bark of a laugh. "No," he agreed. "Not if I really wanted it, of course."

Nneka smiled happily, but Olifur couldn't help but notice the bitterness and sarcasm in Dojhur's voice. He eyed the other boy, but couldn't get any clear idea of what he was thinking. The lantern on the table flickered, the dancing shadows reminding Olifur of how late it had grown.

"I should get back," he said.

"It was lovely seeing you again, Olifur." Nneka leaned over and kissed the top of his head. "Come back and visit me more often."

"I will," he promised.

Dojhur hopped up from the table and offered to walk back to the Platte with him. Sensing that the older boy wanted to discuss something, Olifur accepted.

"Do you really want to come back to the glen with me?" Olifur asked after a little while.

Dojhur did not answer right away. They walked for several blocks in silence before Dojhur spoke, his voice low and earnest. "You have to help me get her away from him."

Olifur found that this did not surprise him as much as it

might have a few hours ago. He looked up into Dojhur's face, his expression unreadable in the darkness. "How? You heard her. She won't leave him."

"And even if she does, he'll just come after her." Dojhur slammed one fist into his open palm. "He'll never just let her go. He'll never let any of us go, no matter what Nneka believes."

"Dojhur," Olifur began, but then he clapped his mouth shut. He still wasn't sure whether he wanted to trust his new friend.

"What is it?"

Olifur hesitated.

"What?"

Olifur made a decision and plunged forward. "What if we could help Nneka see who he truly is?"

"She already knows he's a thief," Dojhur replied in a low snarl. "We all are. Even Nneka's stolen and lied. She's not as pure and perfect as you think."

Olifur stopped mid-stride and swung around to face his friend. "I never said she was perfect."

"You didn't have to. I can see it in your eyes when you look at her. You think she could never do nothing wrong in her life. But she's lied, and she's cheated, and she's stolen. And she did it all for *him*. We all do." Dojhur's voice rang with disgust. "She talks of how he saved her and how he takes care of all of us. Oh yes. He's taken care of us, all right. Taught us his trade. Given us a way to take from a world that won't give us nothing any other way. And we're good at it. He demands perfection, Olifur. I'm *good* at stealing. How else do you think I got my nickname? And more than that, I *like* it. Taking a purse or a bit of jewelry or even someone's fancy silk scarf is like a game. An easy game that I always win. I'm the best there is at this trade. Better than Bale, even. He's too slow for this kind of work. That's why he takes care of all the bigger jobs, breaking into houses or shops. But he always has one of us with him, oh yes, because we're the extra card up his sleeve in his game." Dojhur nodded grimly. "The last task every one of us will do for him is take his noose."

Olifur gaped slightly at the matter-of-fact way Dojhur delivered this information. Then he shook himself. "Dojhur, I have to tell you something."

"What's that?" Dojhur asked, kicking at a stone as they began walking again.

"I met Bale before I came to Melar."

As they passed under the faint glow of a gas lantern, Olifur caught Dojhur's puzzled frown.

"You did? When? Where? He didn't seem to recognize you."

"He wouldn't have," Olifur said. "It was three years ago."

Dojhur tilted his head. "That would explain it. You've probably grown a lot in three years."

"I have," Olifur said solemnly. "A lot."

"So, where did you meet him?" Dojhur pressed.

Olifur took a deep breath. "Bale killed my parents."

16

THE REVELATION

Dojhur stopped in his tracks and stared at Olifur. "What?"
"He killed my parents," Olifur repeated. "Murdered them in cold blood on the road to Melar."

"Are you sure?" Dojhur asked, a muscle twitching in his jaw. He stared fiercely down at Olifur. "Are you sure it was him?"

"I remember it clear as the stars on a cloudless night," Olifur said. "It was three years ago. I was little, but if I close my eyes, I'm there again. I can see it all. My mother was ill. She'd been sick for a long time. I think my father must have talked to every physician within fifty miles, but none of them could help her. He was desperate, and I think he was running out of money. And time. They didn't tell me everything, but I sort of just *knew* that things were getting real bad. He decided to take her to Melar because he'd heard of a physician who he hoped could heal her. We weren't far from the city when Bale and another man he called 'Cuyler' attacked us and stole our leythan and carriage. My father tried to stop them, and Bale stabbed him. He stabbed my mother, too. Then he left me behind to die. I would have died, too, if Fritjof hadn't found me."

A long silence stretched between them. At length, Dojhur gave himself a shake. "He called the other man Cuyler?"

"Yes. And Cuyler called the one in charge 'Bale.'"

"I might not believe you, except that you mentioned Cuyler." The older boy shivered.

"Who's Cuyler?" Olifur ventured.

Dojhur heaved a sigh. "He was Bale's partner in the business."

"Was?"

"He took a crossbow bolt to the side about a year ago." Dojhur shrugged. "Running from the city guards after a heist that went wrong. Bale swore it was Cuyler who killed the old couple they were stealing from... but now..." Dojhur shoved his hands deep in his pockets. "I knew Bale was capable of it," he muttered. "But I didn't realize..." He trailed off. "All the more reason to get Nneka away from him. Hey, when do you think you'll have enough saved up to leave Melar?"

Olifur thought for a moment. "Two sennights. Maybe one if Master Epps stays as generous as he's been."

Dojhur thought about that for a little while, his face squinched up as if puzzling over an intractable problem. "All right. Good to know. I'll have to figure out a way to convince Nneka to come with us, but now that I know about your parents... Maybe she won't believe me. I dunno. But at least we've got a little more time."

They resumed walking, and a few minutes later they had reached the Platte. Dojhur tousled Olifur's hair.

"Hey, do me a favor and stay out of sight for a bit," he said.

"Why?"

"Just... a feeling I've got," Dojhur hedged.

Olifur grimaced at him. "You're gonna have to do better than that."

"Look, ever since he met you, Bale's been talking about figuring out a way to break into the Platte and steal a few cynders. They're worth a sizable sum, more than we've ever seen at once. The only thing that's been stopping him from using you is the fact that you had no access to the cynders. Now that you do..."

"It's not like he knows that," Olifur said.

"True, and I'm not gonna tell him. But... secrets have a way of being found out. Especially by people like Bale. And while Nneka wouldn't hurt you on purpose, she might not realize the consequences of telling Bale. She loves him, Olifur. She can't see him for what he really is. So, please, just... lie low for a while. At least give me a few days to figure some things out."

"All right." Olifur kicked at a pebble. "But I hate the idea of being a prisoner in there." He glanced up at the enormous edifice of the Platte with a grimace.

"I'll swing by next time Bale goes on a longer job and let you know," Dojhur promised. "You can come visit again, then."

"And if you want to come out to the forest with me, be here an hour after sundown in three nights," Olifur said. "And look in on Master Epps for me, would you? He'll give you a biscuit if you sweep his shop out for him at closing time. But you gotta promise not to steal anything from him."

"All right," Dojhur said.

"Promise not to steal from him," Olifur said fiercely.

Dojhur held his hands up and laughed, dancing away slightly. "I promise, I promise!"

"Break your promise and I'll turn you over to Garth myself."

Dojhur's eyebrows shot up. "Ooh. I forgot you had friends in high places, little Olifur. I'm shaking in my boots."

Olifur glanced down pointedly at Dojhur's bare feet and the older boy laughed and hopped up and down on his toes. "Night, Olifur."

"Night, Dojhur."

Olifur mounted the steps and crawled onto his pallet, but for a long time he could not sleep. His thoughts continued to spiral around the problem of Bale and how to get Nneka and Dojhur and the other boys out of his clutches. He wished Fritjof were there with him. The old man would have known what to do. Of course, if Fritjof were healthy enough to be there with him, Olifur never would have come to Melar. He sighed and tossed fitfully, struggling to find a comfortable position on his mattress.

It was early morning before he finally drifted off to sleep, only to be woken rudely by the other boys shouting and thumping their way across the floor in their haste to get to the mess hall for a few bites of barely edible mushy porridge before starting their tasks for the day. Olifur groaned and flopped himself out of bed, blinking blearily in the gray light of pre-dawn. Outside, thunder rumbled ominously and he could hear the pitter-pat of raindrops on the window ledge. His heart sank. Rain made everything about the Platte more slippery and treacherous. It also tended to make Hughin more irritable than usual.

Stumbling along in the mad rush of bodies, he joined the line of hungry boys and held his bowl up to receive his meager portion. He sat at a long table and aimlessly swirled his spoon around in the gray sludge. His stomach growled, but he couldn't quite bring himself to eat the porridge. Most mornings he forced himself to, knowing he needed to eat, but today everything seemed dull and lusterless.

"You gonna eat that?" the boy next to him asked, his own bowl already licked clean.

Olifur suddenly remembered that he had a saffron bun from Master Epps tucked in his pocket from the previous night. He had meant to give it to Nneka, but had forgotten. Without a word, he slid his bowl to the other boy. He rose and scanned the room until he caught sight of Sven, then made his way over to the much older boy.

"If it's all right with you, I thought I'd go get started," Olifur said.

The older boy looked up, and a sly grin crossed his face. "Sure." He tossed the key to the shed at Olifur. "I'll be right down."

Olifur knew from experience that this meant Sven would take his time over breakfast, possibly spend some long, leisurely minutes chatting with the cook, and pause on his way out the door to flirt with Sooki in hopes of an extra stin here and there, but he had long since stopped caring about the older boy's laziness. As the overseer of the loading crew, Sven was safe from Hughin's cane, and any word one of the smaller boys dared voice against him would merely be seen as whining, or worse, mutiny. Olifur comforted himself with the thought that he only had to put up with it for a while longer. Two more sennights, maybe less, and he would be gone from Melar and free from the Platte forever.

He ambled slowly out of the mess and down the stairs, munching surreptitiously on the sweet roll. Even after spending a night in his pocket, it tasted delicious, a perfect blend of sweet and savory. Outside, the rain drizzled steadily. As he crossed the muddy yard to the shed, it coated his hair and dripped down his face and neck into his collar. His toes squelched in the wet grass as he crossed to the shed. He unlocked the door, pocketed the key, picked up the first cynder, and trekked back across the yard to the building and up the stairs.

Olifur had only made two trips before the other boys on the crew finally joined him. They worked together in miserable silence, their entire focus on the task before them.

It was a relief to finish the last trip up the steps, but then Sven ordered them to go back downstairs and wash the mud from their feet and legs. When they had finished that, he handed them buckets and sponges and told them to clean the stairs and the floors where they had tracked mud, and when they finished with that, they had to wash again before he would let them get started on their regular chore of cleaning and polishing the interior of the train.

As the day turned into evening and the hours wore on, Olifur found himself accidentally dozing off while washing the inside of the train's windows. He jerked himself awake, blinking furiously and shaking his head, but the scant hours of sleep from the previous night had caught up with him, and he drifted in and out of consciousness. He pinched himself and slapped himself across the face, but he could not stave off the exhaustion.

Hughin's cane slammed down on his shoulder, startling him

painfully back to full wakefulness, and he began polishing the brass fittings on the seat in front of him vigorously.

"You've polished that same seat three times," Hughin barked. "I've been watching you."

"I'm sorry, sir," Olifur said. He tried to edge around the man to the next row, but Hughin blocked him with a ferocious scowl.

"Sven said you started early today," Hughin growled.

"I..." Olifur's tired brain tried to process how he should respond to the accusation, but he couldn't think of anything appropriately contrite.

"He said you didn't stop for meals, either."

"I'm sorry?"

"We don't pay you more for working through your breaks, you know."

"I know," Olifur replied dully. He could never explain to this man why he needed to throw himself into his work today: to forget the terrible memories of his parents' deaths, to stop reliving the worst moments of his life, to take his mind off of its spiraling descent into madness as he tried to figure out a way to help his new friends get away from a man he knew to be a murderer. With a sigh, he once again tried to dart around the man, but Hughin clasped him by the shoulder.

"Get on then and finish your job," Hughin said gruffly. The man turned and stumped away. "If I find you sleeping on this train, you'll never work here another day. I'll toss you out on the street meself."

It didn't take long for Olifur to finish. The threat of losing his job and any hope of steady wages was enough to keep his eyelids from drooping again until he finally fell into his bed.

The next day was even more miserable, and by the end of it, Olifur felt ready to explode like a dropped cynder. The other boys had been more than usually rude and mocking in their interactions with him, and Hughin's cane had bitten into his back with more frequency and force than usual. Nothing he did was good enough or fast enough or smart enough. The food in the mess tasted more like mud than usual. No matter where he looked, all he saw was gray and colorless and cruel.

Two more sennights. Two more sennights. The thought pounded through his mind with a comforting steadiness, keeping him from barking at the other boys, preventing him from grabbing Hughin's cane and rapping him sharply with it to see how he liked such treatment. But at the end of the day, he could bear it no longer. Despite his promise to Dojhur, he felt he must escape from this wretched place or go mad. He wouldn't stay out long, he promised himself. And he wouldn't go near any of Nneka's normal haunts. But he had to leave. He had to get away. And he couldn't bear the thought of two more sennights in this place, not when he might earn a couple of extra stin from Master Epps and his friends and get out of Melar sooner, get back to Fritjof, the other boys, and the glen. The walls of the Platte loomed over him, closing in around him with choking, squeezing pressure; it would soon crush him if he didn't get out, even for just an hour or two.

17

ABDUCTED!

The darkness of the night enfolded Olifur in its arms, welcoming him like a long-lost friend as he stepped outside the Platte and onto the street. Dusk greeted him in a haze of gray and violet that darkened by the minute. Mist swirled up from the ground, flushing with an eerie, parchment-colored glow as a man sitting atop a tall pole outside the Platte lit the gas lamp. Olifur gave a wave to the man atop the ladder and the man waved back with his polishing rag, before shimmying down the ladder and setting off for the next lantern on his route.

Olifur crept through the city cautiously, keeping one eye out for familiar faces, but he made it to Hildy's without incident. Master Epps confirmed Dojhur had stopped by to sweep the previous night.

"Didn't much like the look of him at first," Epps confided. "But he dropped your name, and he did a real nice job once I showed him how. Nothing went missing after he left, either."

Olifur grinned. "I'm having a good influence, I think," he joked, then he sobered. "Or perhaps he's seen for himself how hard work and the best-tasting rolls in town make for a delightful combination."

Master Epps's eyes twinkled in pleasure at the compliment

and he handed over an apple crown when Olifur finished sweeping out the shop. Olifur thought he had never tasted anything so good in his whole life. The fresh air, the soft glow of the lanterns in the mist, the conversation with Master Epps, and the sweet treat reminded him that the world was not all darkness and despair.

As he meandered along, taking bites of the tart and flaky apple crown, someone suddenly grabbed him roughly from behind. Before he even had a chance to shout, a scratchy sack slammed down over his head, obscuring his vision. The pastry dropped to the ground. Olifur kicked and fought, trying to shout through the sack and his mouthful of dessert, but whoever held him captive had a grip like iron, and he knew his muffled protests wouldn't travel far. Still, he fought as hard as he could. He felt his foot connect with something and heard a soft grunt of pain. Then something hard slammed against the side of his head and the world went black.

Olifur woke blinking in a dark room with a single candle giving off a faint glow from somewhere above him. His head throbbed viciously, and he squeezed his eyes shut, trying to block out the pain or diminish it. He lay on his side on a hard floor of packed dirt, and his hands were bound behind him with ropes tied so tightly his fingers were tingling as though someone were stabbing them with thousands of tiny needles. At least there was no longer anything over his head and face, not that he could see anything, anyway.

"Now, let's go over the plan again." Harsh whispers traveled to his ears, but he couldn't make out who was speaking.

"What if he doesn't go along with it?"

"If he knows what's good for him, he will."

"He isn't a thief. I don't think you can force him." This voice was a bit louder than a whisper, and Olifur thought it sounded vaguely familiar, but his head ached so fiercely that he couldn't focus on figuring it out.

"All I need is for him to get us into the shed. He doesn't have to do any of the actual stealing."

"Bale..."

"Shh! He's awake."

Olifur felt himself being lifted painfully off the ground by rough hands that set him down in a chair. He blinked up into the familiar faces of Bale, Dojhur, and one of the other boys from the cellar whose name Olifur hadn't caught. Dojhur stared at him with wide, frightened eyes, but Olifur was still having a hard time focusing on anything through the throbbing in his head.

Bale filled his field of vision, blocking his view of the other boys as he leaned over Olifur. "Well now, friend," he said in a genial tone. "Sorry about all that. Dojhur here seemed to think you wouldn't be amenable to having a little chat with us. But you're a reasonable sort, right?"

Olifur blinked at him.

Bale sneered. "All I want is my fair share, my due. And you're going to help me get it."

"How?" Olifur rasped, his throat suddenly dry as he realized where he was.

"Dojhur here tells me you've been recently promoted, and congratulations are in order," Bale said.

Over his shoulder, Dojhur was making some frantic expressions with his eyes, but Olifur couldn't see him properly as Bale's shoulder and face kept getting in the way. His heart sank. So then Dojhur had just been using him after all.

"So?" Olifur hissed through clenched teeth.

"So that means you now have access to some precious materials."

"The brass polish?" Olifur asked, unable to stop himself.

"Don't think you're smart," Bale exploded, looming up over him with a menacing flash in his eyes. "You know what I'm after. The cynders, boy. A man could set himself up like a king with just a few of those precious little rocks."

"They're not really all that little." Olifur knew he was playing with a rabid dog, but he couldn't help himself. The throbbing pain and the sense of betrayal and danger as he faced his parents' murderer were mixing strangely together in his brain and he felt like he couldn't quite control his words.

He expected the man to backhand him across the face, but Bale merely scowled down at him in confusion. "Eh? What do you mean?"

Olifur stared at him. "Haven't you ever seen one?"

A brief silence reigned, and the flicker of an idea tickled the back of Olifur's mind as he took in Bale's confused expression.

"You haven't, have you?" he asked. "I'm losing the feeling in my hands. If you cut the ropes, I'll tell you all about the cynders."

Bale scowled at him.

"Where am I gonna go?" Olifur asked, trying to look small and helpless, playing into the man's need to be in control. "Pretty sure I can't get out of here unless you let me."

Bale's lips pursed up and then he gave a brief nod to Dojhur, who moved around behind Olifur and started sawing at the ropes around his hands.

"I didn't tell him, Oli. Honest," he breathed into Olifur's ear.

Olifur gave no sign that he'd heard. But something tight in his heart eased as the ropes loosened. He flexed his fingers a few times before rubbing at his sore wrists.

"They're not small," Olifur said, staring straight into Bale's eyes and holding his hands apart to demonstrate. "The cynders. They're big. Bigger than a large loaf of bread. And heavy. And you have to carry them in special crates so they don't jostle around because if one gets jostled too much..." He trailed off and widened his eyes as he shrugged his shoulders as expressively as he could. "Boom."

"I know all about the rumors and myths." Bale waved a dismissive hand. "Aren't they supposed to glow like they're lit with an inner fire, too?" His tone dripped with sarcasm, and Olifur latched onto it, remembering the conversation he had overheard between Bale and Nneka.

"Oh, dear." Olifur laughed as derisively as he could manage. "You've heard that story? Isn't it ridiculous? Probably made up by one of those hearthfire idiots who believes the cynders are *magical*." He emphasized the last word with as much scorn as he could muster, then he paused and glanced at Bale out of the corner of his eye, holding his breath.

The ploy worked. Bale snorted. "Magic don't exist," he scoffed.

"Of course it doesn't," Olifur agreed. "That's just a word people use when they're too embarrassed to admit they don't understand something. Right?"

Bale nodded. "So what do they look like?" Bale asked, curiosity and greed in his every syllable.

"They're gray and made of a special ore," Olifur said, thinking as fast as he could. "And shaped sort of like cylinders, but they're not round; they're hexagons at the top and bottom. The boys at the Platte say that they really can explode if they're dropped, though. Something about how they store energy and power and that's what makes the trains run."

Bale's eyes gleamed. "And they're worth a fortune." He licked his lips. "Here is what we're going to do, lads. In a few hours, we'll have Olifur here show us where they keep these cynders. We'll break in and take what we want." He paused, frowning as Olifur shook his head frantically. "What?" he snapped in irritation.

"If you can wait until tomorrow night, I can get you all the cynders you can carry, easy."

"I suppose I'd have to let you go, eh?" Bale narrowed his eyes suspiciously.

"Yeah." Olifur shrugged, thinking fast, doing calculations in his head. "But if you try to break in tonight, you'll get caught. They store the cynders up on the top floor of the Platte," he lied. "They're heavily guarded. You'd have to sneak by all the dorms full of sleeping workers and overseers to get in and out. That'd be hard to do without making a lot of noise. But tomorrow, I could bring some cynders down to one of the storage sheds. No guards, no doors to break down, just a little walk across the yard and you're as wealthy as you've ever dreamed." He held his breath, hoping Bale would believe him.

"That easy?" Bale asked.

"Well, easy for you. I'll have to be pretty careful, and if I get caught, I'll lose my job. Possibly get locked up for good."

"And why should I trust you? Why would you be willing to take that kind of risk and rob your employer for me?"

Olifur twisted sideways and yanked the collar of his shirt down, showing off the fresh bruises on his back and shoulders from Hughin's cane. "Why wouldn't I be willing?" he growled, letting all the bitterness of his situation flood his voice. He gave Bale a fierce glare.

Bale crossed his arms and stared at him. Olifur kept his gaze steady, resisting the urge to glance away or look at Dojhur. His heart pounded in his ears and he was certain the villain would hear it and know that this was all a lie.

"All right," the man finally said. "We'll try it your way. But if you run or try to double-cross me, I'll wring your miserable neck and leave you in the gutter and won't nobody shed a tear for your corpse."

Olifur tried to hold back the sudden need to swallow and look away, but he couldn't quite manage it. He hunched his shoulders, suddenly chilled through. "I can go, then?" he asked.

"Dojhur, the blindfold," Bale barked.

Dojhur shot Olifur an apologetic glance before shoving the burlap sack back down over his head.

"Do this job right, and I might have a place for you on my crew," Bale growled. "We'll be outside the Platte at midnight tomorrow. Don't disappoint me."

Olifur shook his head wordlessly and allowed himself to be led outside. Dojhur led him along, spinning him around several times and turning multiple corners before he lifted the sack from Olifur's head.

"Look." Dojhur spoke quickly, as if trying to stave off any

accusations. "I didn't tell Bale about your new job. I swear. I was trying to keep you safe. I warned you to lie low."

"Yeah." Olifur rubbed at his wrists, not wanting to think about who must have informed Bale. He told himself that Nneka didn't know what she was doing, but he found that the excuse plunked hollowly in his thoughts.

Dojhur squinted at him. "You have a plan, don't you?"

"Why do you say that?" Olifur asked, not quite ready to trust again.

Dojhur's expression fell. "Just... be careful, right? You know how dangerous he is. And if he ever found out you crossed him..."

"Maybe I'm just tired of the Platte and hate Hughin that much," Olifur countered.

Dojhur screwed up one side of his face. "Maybe so. But I don't believe it."

"How come?"

"Because..." Dojhur paused. "I can't quite explain it."

Olifur decided not to press the older boy. "You're right. I do have a plan. But I'll have to leave Melar tomorrow night when it's all finished," he said. "You can still come with me."

Even in the faint glow of the lantern light, Olifur could see Dojhur's face grow pale.

"Bale..."

"I'm going to make sure he can't follow us," Olifur said. "Trust me. Just make sure he comes in person to get the cynders."

"That shouldn't be too hard," Dojhur mused. "This whole idea has made him a little insane. I can push him a little more off balance about it so he won't trust the job to anyone else."

"Good."

"But I thought you needed another sennight or two to earn enough coin for the doctor? How can you be ready to leave already?"

Olifur sighed. "I'm just hoping that the doctor will agree to come for a little less than he asked for. After this is done, I can't stay here. If the plan doesn't work, or if Bale gets away..." He trailed off. Perhaps Fritjof had gotten better on his own. Or perhaps the doctor would already be too late. Maybe Bale would get locked up for good and Olifur could stay and earn the rest of the sum he needed. "I have to plan for the worst."

Dojhur made a face and dug in his pocket. "Here." He held out a handful of small coins. "If you're serious about letting me come back to the glen with you..."

Olifur hesitated.

As if reading his thoughts, Dojhur gave a self-conscious little chuckle. "It's not stolen, if that's what you're worried about."

"It's not?" Olifur asked, startled, and feeling suddenly a little bit bad about being startled.

Dojhur's mouth twisted in a crooked grin. "I took that advice you gave me the first time we met and tried some honest work."

"Doing what?" Olifur asked, unable to think of anything else to say.

"Helping the fishermen untangle their nets. They pay pretty good."

"That's... that's good."

"What else do you need?" Dojhur asked.

Olifur's thoughts raced ahead to the next night. There were several things he needed to do before he could sleep, yet, but one thing weighed on his heart. It was something he couldn't put off any longer.

"Dojhur, I need to talk to Nneka. Now. Without Bale anywhere nearby."

"I don't think that's a good idea..."

"Please, Dojhur."

Dojhur shuffled his feet a bit, then relented. "I might be able to manage it. Can you find your way down to the docks?"

"Yes."

"Go on down there and wait. If we're not there in an hour, we're not coming."

Olifur nodded, and they parted ways. He trotted down the muddy streets, avoiding puddles as best he could, until he reached the sandy shore. A pier jutted out over the ocean, and tiny fishing boats bobbed up and down in the bay. He had not made it down to the ocean yet in his explorations of the city, though he knew that much of Melar's business revolved around the fisherman's trade. Nneka did not come here, and he had been so captivated by her sweet smile that he had never strayed too far from her usual routes. Now he inhaled the fresh, strong wild scents of the ocean and stared out at the water stretching endlessly to the horizon, with the moonlight sparkling on its rippling back. With a start, he realized that the constant thunder he had always been only vaguely aware of while in the city came from the waves pounding up on the shore. He dug his toes into the soft sand—still warm and sun-baked even in the gathering darkness—and grinned, for a moment forgetting all about Bale and the cynders in his sudden joy at this new discovery. He gazed out at the little boats and marveled at the courage of their unknown captains. To think that they trusted their lives to such tiny crafts as they voyaged out each day, skimming the surface of such vast and terrible depths! He admired them, these unknown men, and wished he had come here sooner. He would have liked to meet them, perhaps learn from them that kind of courage.

"Olifur?"

The soft voice made him turn. Nneka stood before him, her skirt and scarf billowing in the ocean breeze, moonlight falling around her golden hair like a gentle embrace.

"Nneka," he greeted her solemnly. "I have to tell you something."

"Dojhur said that Bale is trying to pull you into one of his schemes," she cried, forestalling what he had been about to say. She took a step toward him, hands outstretched. "Oh, Olifur, you mustn't! You should go, get out of this city, away from this place. One of the fishermen here is a friend of mine. He will hide you on his boat and take you down the coast out of Bale's clutches. Please, don't let him..." She faltered, tears glistening on her cheeks. "Don't let him ruin you, too."

Olifur stared at her, his mouth hanging slightly open. It was so different from what he had expected; he didn't know exactly what to say.

"Nneka?" He stepped closer to her. "Did you tell him I was working with the cynders?"

Her eyes widened, and she startled backwards. "Olifur! How could you think that?" She shook her head violently, her hair flying in every direction; the wind caught it and flung it across her face and she had to dig strands of it out of her mouth. "I didn't tell him."

"Then who?"

"I don't know. But knowing Bale, I'm sure he has friends inside the Platte. At this point, it don't matter who told him. He found out and now he's got this insane idea in his head, and he just—he won't be stopped. You have to get out of here. You have to get away from him."

"Come with me."

She stared at him. "I couldn't. What would I do without him? Oh, I hate him so. No. No, that's a wicked thing to say. I love him. I love him. And he needs me."

"Nneka, you don't know what he's done."

"You don't know what I've done," she retorted. "I don't have any choice anymore. Maybe I did once, before he found me, before he caught me in his web of lies and theft. But I'm caught now, Olifur. He rescued me, took me in, taught me. Now I'm the one protecting him from being any worse than he is."

"He's already worse than you know, Nneka."

She shook her head, the denial springing to her lips, but Olifur could not stop now. No matter how cruel it might be, he had to say it, had to tell her.

"He murdered my parents, Nneka."

She took a step back, shaking her head. "No. He couldn't have. He wouldn't do such a thing. You must be remembering wrong. You said your parents died three years ago. You were so little..."

"It's true," Olifur cut her off. "Bale and a man named Cuyler stole our carriage and murdered my parents on the road to Melar. They left me in the road to die. I might have been little, but I remember their faces. Their voices. Their names. The second I looked into Bale's face in your cellar, I knew him, Nneka. I could never forget that face. The face that laughed as my parents lay bleeding in the road and said he was leaving me for the grymstalkers."

Nneka stared at him wordlessly. The crashing of the waves and the whipping wind were the only sounds, and they thundered in Olifur's ears like his own blood. He held his breath, knowing he had hurt her but also knowing that he couldn't have done differently. She deserved to know the truth.

"C-Cuyler?" she finally stammered. "Where... where did you hear that name?"

"That's what Bale called the man he was with when they ambushed our carriage," Olifur said grimly. "I bit him on the leg."

Nneka laughed, a hollow, hopeless sound quickly swallowed up by the roaring surf. She covered her face with her hands and her shoulders shook for a moment. Then she looked up, her lips pressed firmly into a line, tears shimmering in her eyes. "I can't save him, can I?"

Her words were so small, so forlorn. Olifur darted forward and wrapped his arms tightly around her waist. She seemed startled for a moment, then she embraced him back, her chin resting briefly on the top of his head.

He stepped back and looked up at her. "Please come with us."

She smiled sadly, then turned and stared out at the ocean. "Perhaps I could..."

"We're leaving tomorrow night," Olifur said. "Dojhur knows the time and place."

18

DARKNESS OF NIGHT

{

It was well past midnight before Olifur finally returned to his bed. Despite his exhaustion, he lay on his pallet and stared up at the ceiling for a long time before he finally drifted off to sleep. In his dreams, someone shoved a dark hood over his head. Nneka screamed. Dojhur swung from a gallows. And rough hands shook him and shoved him, making him drop his precious handful of stin and the coins bounced and slithered into the gutter while he scrabbled frantically to catch them and hold them up to the physician, pleading that he save Fritjof's life, but Doctor Sveljen just shook his head sadly at the meager offering and turned away.

Morning came far too early, but the horrible nightmares and the nervous fluttering in his stomach propelled him out of bed without complaint. He raced through his breakfast, barely tasting the sludgy porridge, before sauntering over to Sven and offering to get started on the loading. Sven tossed him the key to the shed without even bothering to look up from his bowl, and Olifur hurried down the stairs. He resisted the urge to look over his shoulder, knowing that if he acted strangely, it would draw attention. Nothing strange about Olifur starting work before the other boys. That was a fairly normal enough occurrence.

By the time Sven and the other boys showed up to help, Olifur had made little progress on his regular duties, other than bringing down all the empty cynders.

"You got rocks in your shoes today, Olifur?" Sven complained as he lifted a crate. "You didn't finish half what you usually get done by this time. Why didn't you take any of the live cynders up?" The older boy stared at the stack of empty cynders in bafflement. "Then you would have had crates to put these into. We do this every day. What were you thinking?"

"Didn't sleep well," Olifur mumbled, allowing a real yawn to escape.

He had, in fact, already moved six of the full cynders upstairs, but instead of putting them on the train, he had hidden them in the closet, removing them from their crates and stacking them carefully under a pile of old rags. The empty crates were now sitting behind the shed, the cart that came to take them having already passed by before breakfast. Olifur thanked the Builder that the store of full cynders was so low, they only had twenty-four of them left—enough to get them through this day's trains with only six left over—and weren't due to receive a new shipment until the next morning. He had hidden the extra six cynders, wanting to ensure that Bale could not get his hands on a single one.

The previous night, before he had gone to bed, he had dragged the crates full of empty cynders back into the shed so that the man who came by with a cart each morning to take them away wouldn't get them. He had hoped that the cart driver would simply think there had been a miscommunication and wouldn't try to talk to Hughin about it, and that was exactly what had happened.

"Don't care. Get a move on or I'll get Hughin down here to put a hop in your jump," Sven barked.

"I brought down some empties," Olifur whined.

Sven just shook his head and aimed a kick in Olifur's direction, which he accepted meekly. Olifur made a show of speeding up his efforts, even though his muscles felt like they had turned into the porridge served to him every morning.

At the end of the day, Olifur offered to straighten up the shed, and Sven gave him a disbelieving look. For a moment, Olifur held his breath, afraid he'd pushed too far. But Sven only shrugged.

"You sure enjoy work more than anyone I've ever met," he commented. "Don't you go waking me up later to give me the key. Just keep it. You're the one who unlocks the door every morning, anyway."

Hardly daring to believe that things were working out so well, Olifur merely gave a tired nod and hurried to finish his polishing. With that task completed, he went back out to the shed and brought the six boxes of newly emptied cynders back inside the shed and began rearranging the crates that now held only empty rocks. With two days' worth of cynders, there were twelve crates. He hoped Bale would be satisfied.

Finished with his work and exhausted to his bones, Olifur locked the shed, deposited the key in his pocket, and then slipped away from the Platte. He had two errands to run before everything would be in readiness for the night's main event.

———

THE NIGHT SKY held a patchwork of thin clouds that moved swiftly, blown by a relentless wind. The moon's light shone down in spurts and patches as the clouds shifted before it in an endless dance. Olifur lay on his bed, waiting until he heard the breathing of his roommates turn slow and steady. He waited a while longer, letting them fall into deeper sleep before he rose and tiptoed quietly across the room.

Upon reaching the ground floor, he slipped out through the front door and around the side of the building, where he sat down on a pile of old timbers and waited.

The minutes dragged by. Olifur felt his eyelids growing heavy, and he hopped up from his post and paced to keep himself awake. He needed to be alert when Bale arrived.

But Bale didn't arrive.

The clouds drifted away, blown apart by a gentle breeze. The moon—paler and thinner than the night before, no longer quite full—made its slow arc overhead. Olifur squinted. The moon's sudden light without the diffusion of the clouds seemed dangerously bright and he wished for a darker night. Too much light was not wanted for tonight's activities. Midnight came and went, and Olifur grew worried. Had something stopped the fiend? Had the plan gone awry somehow? Had someone tipped Bale off? Were Dojhur and Nneka safe? Had Nneka somehow warned Bale? He had been careful not to tell her anything that would jeopardize this evening's activities. Had Dojhur said something?

And then he knew. It had been he who had jeopardized this night. An icy hand wrapped around his heart with a deadly grip as terrible knowledge dawned.

He had told Nneka about his parents.

What if she had told Bale who he was? Surely that would give the man pause. He wouldn't show up to complete a job if he suspected that Olifur knew what he was.

A wild terror rose within him. He whirled in the yard. A sudden desperate need to see Nneka, to know if she was all right, filled his entire being. The plan had failed. Bale knew who he was. Everything was collapsing around him, but perhaps it was not too late to save Nneka.

Whirling, Olifur took two swift steps toward the front of the building when someone hissed at him from the thick hedge that surrounded the Platte. He paused, his heart racing wildly in his ears, and peered into the tangled growth.

Bale emerged, his tall, thin frame unfolding as he stood and stepped into the yard. He held up a hooded lantern. In the combination of lantern light and moonlight, his face looked gaunt and sickly. His head swiveled on his neck, nervously looking this way and that. Dojhur trotted along a few steps behind the man, his expression troubled. Olifur wondered what was wrong.

Bale's lip curled up in a sneer as he advanced upon the boy with menacing steps. Olifur forced himself to stand still as the man approached, glad of the darkness that would hide most of the terror he felt in the murderer's presence.

"You're late." Olifur rasped the accusation.

"Got held up," Bale snarled. Perspiration glinted on his forehead. "Get the cart," he snapped at Dojhur.

"What took you so long?" Olifur whispered at Dojhur, who shrugged.

Bale whirled on them both. "Nneka didn't want me to come. Said it was too dangerous and that I shouldn't 'corrupt' someone as young as you. She always could get a little carried away by her emotions." Bale wiped a hand across his mouth and Olifur noticed with horror that the backs of Bale's fingers glistened with something wet and dark.

"Oh?" he asked, trying to sound nonchalant but unable to force any further words from between suddenly numb lips. He threw a panicked glance at Dojhur, who stared back at him with wide, frightened eyes. The older boy looked up at Bale, his face going pale.

"Bale. No." Dojhur's horrified whisper was barely audible. "You—you didn't..."

Bale whirled. "Shut your mouth!" he hissed. "Or I'll do you just like I did her." He drew a knife out of his belt and brandished it threateningly. Dojhur shrank back and clamped his mouth shut, his face turning ghostly in the faint light. Satisfied that he would get no arguments from that quarter, Bale returned his attention to Olifur. "Now, where are these cynders, boy? Be quick. We haven't got all night. Dojhur, bring the wagon." Bale's voice rose in pitch as he spoke.

Olifur stared at the blade in sudden terror, suddenly transported back once again to that day, that dusty road outside of Melar. He stood frozen, unable to move. His thoughts screamed at him to do something, but he could only stare at that knife. He wasn't sure it was the same knife Bale had used that day, but it rested in the same hand that had killed his parents, and suddenly he couldn't move, couldn't breathe. Nneka... His heart wailed her name, but his lips remained clamped shut, his voice frozen in fear.

Dojhur shrank back into the bushes. A moment later, they heard the pounding of retreating footsteps. Bale growled angrily under his breath but did not raise his voice to shout after Dojhur. Nor did he move to follow the boy. He merely fingered his knife thoughtfully before sliding it into its sheath and trudging back into the bushes to retrieve the cart himself. It was a long, shallow, rectangular thing that rolled on noiseless wheels.

"Useless boy," Bale muttered. "I'll take care of him later." He turned his gaze on Olifur, a strange light in his eyes. "You open that shed like you promised, or I'll wring your neck right here. Won't nobody care, neither."

Choking back his despair at Dojhur's sudden abandonment of their plan and his terror for Nneka, as well as for himself, Olifur led him to the little shed. With trembling fingers, he inserted the key in the lock—it took him several tries—and turned it, swinging the door open. Bale shoved past him into the dark interior, his head swinging this way and that. A little moonlight streamed in through the small window high in the wooden walls, preventing the room from being utterly black.

"Over there." Olifur pointed at the crates he had carefully prepared for the evening's activities.

Bale lifted a crowbar off the rack of tools and pried open a crate. He lifted the lantern and peered inside, where, nestled in a cocoon of straw, sat one of the empty gray cynders. Bale's teeth glinted as his mouth stretched into a smile of greedy exultation.

"Quick, boy, put this one in the wagon," he snapped, setting the lantern down on a workbench.

Olifur obeyed wordlessly, grief roiling in the pit of his stomach. He must not think of Nneka, he told himself. There would be time to mourn later. He worked slowly, trying to give the rest of his plan time to unfold.

Bale grabbed another crate, following right on Olifur's heels, nearly tripping over him in his haste. He snapped at the boy about moving faster and then went back into the shed. Outside, Olifur deposited the crate into the waiting cart, then returned to the shed for another crate. Quietly, he counted the seconds. When would Garth arrive? Why wasn't he here yet?

They worked in silence. Olifur's already-tired arms felt like unbaked dough. His muscles shook every time he went to lift another crate, and after a few trips to the cart, he didn't even have to pretend to move slowly. Bale's movements grew more and more frenetic. Olifur noticed the man's labored breathing, the way his head jerked up at every new sound. The man's edginess grew, and he snarled threats and curses under his breath every time Olifur lagged or fumbled his grip on a crate. The minutes ticked by slowly, and the cart filled up faster than he wanted. Finally, the last crate was on the pile.

Bale scanned the interior of the storage shed. "What about up there?" He pointed at the smaller crates along the back wall.

Olifur shrugged wearily. "Just the latest shipment of polishing cloths," he said, sinking down to sit against the wall, grateful that he had moved the extra live cynders upstairs and out of Bale's reach already.

Bale narrowed his eyes and bent down to peer into Olifur's face. The boy didn't even flinch at the man's nearness, his exhaustion all-too real.

"Is that so?" he sneered.

Retrieving the pry bar, Bale stalked over to the crates and levered the lid off one at random. With an exultant hiss, he swiped his hand through the cloths. Finding nothing of value, Bale swung around and glared down at Olifur.

"All of these just for rags?" he demanded, brandishing the pry bar.

Olifur nodded wearily. "The trains need a lot of polishing," he said. "Inside and out. There's all that brass and gold. Some of the inlays are even sterling silver." He regretted the words as soon as they were out of his mouth. Bale's eyes gleamed as he glanced up at the sleeping train.

"Are they, now?"

No! Olifur wanted to kick himself. How could he have been so stupid? Where was Garth? He could not take Bale inside the Platte; it would ruin the entire plan. Before he could think of a way to backtrack his words, however, Bale had grabbed him by his collar and hauled him upright, thrusting him through the doorway and out into the yard again.

"Show me," he growled.

Olifur's collar dug into his throat, and he frantically shook his head. "I don't have the key." He gasped the lie, hoping it would turn the man aside.

Bale shoved him forward, and he fell painfully to his knees on the ground, landing on the hard gravel path. "Then get out of my way."

The man hooked the pry bar onto his belt and stalked past, leaving Olifur kneeling on the ground behind him. Olifur wanted to call out, to stop him, but he couldn't think of anything to say that wouldn't get him killed. Bale reached the door and carefully pushed it open. The interior of the Platte yawned darkly at them. The man made as though to step across the threshold.

"Bale." A quavering, beautiful voice rang out across the yard.

Olifur's head jerked up as Bale froze, his hand still on the knob. As Olifur watched, the man's shoulders hunched and then —slowly, oh, so slowly!—Bale turned away from the building toward the voice. His face turned ghostly pale in the moonlight as he caught sight of the speaker. Olifur chanced turning his head to look and see what Bale had seen.

There, standing just a few feet away, draped in a flowing white gown and silhouetted in silver moonlight, her pale hair hanging in graceful curls about her shoulders, stood Nneka. She was deathly pale, and large, dark stains marred the front of her dress. Trembling, she reached out her arms to Bale, and the man shrank back at the sight of those pale, delicate hands covered in blood.

"Bale…" The woman's voice held a pleading note in its gentle tones. "Bale…" she gasped and doubled over, holding her stomach.

"No!" Bale's voice shuddered. He took a hasty step backward, colliding with the door in a painful-sounding crash. "Get back! Haunt me not! It was an accident, I tell you! An accident!"

"Halt!" A new voice boomed out through the night air, and Olifur felt himself go limp with relief at Garth's familiar baritone. "In the name of the city guard!"

Bale's eyes, already wild at the sight of Nneka's ghost, grew huge and frantic. His head whipped about as he sought a safe exit.

"We have you surrounded!" Garth's voice shouted again.

"Bale…" Nneka's fragile voice seemed to push him over the edge.

Bale's frenzied gaze fastened on Olifur, still kneeling on the ground just a few steps away. With a bound, the man caught him up roughly and pressed the blade of his knife to Olifur's throat.

"Stay away!" he screamed into the darkness. "Stay away or I kill the boy!"

"Put him down," Garth commanded. "Drop your weapon."

"No!" Bale shouted, his voice cracking with hysteria. He backed toward the building, dragging Olifur with him.

Olifur tried to twist out of the man's grasp, kicking at his shins with his heels, but the knife blade bit painfully into his neck, so he went still.

"Bale!" Nneka called. "Please…" Her plea cut off with a gurgling cough and she fell to her knees.

"You stay away from me," Bale screamed, brandishing the knife at her. "I didn't want to kill you, Nneka! You made me do it!

You made me do it!" His words burst from his throat in anguished, screaming sobs. "Get away!"

Nneka lifted her head and stared at him. Her lips moved, but no sound came out.

"No!" Bale let loose an unearthly shriek. With a burst of speed, he dragged Olifur through the doors of the Platte, slamming them behind them, cutting them off from Garth and the rest of the city guards.

19

DARKNESS OF SOUL

Inside the Platte, Bale shoved Olifur away from him and jammed the pry bar under the door. He stood still, panting heavily. His eyes were wild, and he ran a hand roughly through his hair.

"That will stop them," he muttered. "But it won't stop *her*. They say ghosts can walk right through walls. Oh!" He shoved his fingers into his hair and yanked, making the dark strands stick out wildly. He gazed at Olifur as though staring right through him.

A pounding sounded on the door. Bale lunged for Olifur and pressed his blade to the boy's throat.

"Up the stairs," he snarled, and began backing up the steps into the shadowy darkness of the Platte.

Olifur stumbled and tripped over his own feet as the man dragged him up the stairs. His thoughts were frantic. He desperately needed to get away, to get Bale out of the Platte, to check on Nneka. She needed a doctor. Was she even still alive? Why had she risked her life to come here for him? He shuddered as he remembered the blood glistening wet and dark in the fragile moonlight.

Below, the pounding on the door continued, but now they had reached the door leading out onto the train deck. Bale slipped through the door. Olifur heard a sound like breaking wood, and felt his heart leap, but Bale pulled him out onto the deck and stared around wildly, his grip around Olifur's throat never lessening.

Thumping sounded below, feet pounding up the stairs after them. Bale growled something low and deep in his throat, and then he backed out onto the train road. Olifur felt his heart race, his palms growing sweaty with fear at the height. Bale stared down between the treads of the great road, his breathing quick and sharp in Olifur's ear.

Olifur wanted to fight. To scream at the man. To run away. But the man's grip around him was like a band of iron and the knife bit painfully into his skin. Bale wouldn't hesitate to slit his throat and let him fall; he knew that. The exhaustion and fear mingled together, making his thoughts muzzy and confused.

The door to the deck burst open, and several guards came through, Garth leading them. He stopped when he saw Bale out on the tracks, Olifur still firmly in his grip.

"I'll kill the boy," Bale hissed.

"Hold on, now," Garth began, his voice calm. "There's no need for all of this. Just let the boy go."

Olifur whimpered as Bale thrust him forward by his collar. His feet scrabbled for purchase on the slippery surface of the raised track.

"All of you, back away!" Bale snarled. "Back away, or I push him off this road."

Garth raised his hands, signaling to his men to take a step back. "Easy now..."

"Bale! Let him go!" Dojhur's voice rang out as the young thief slipped between the guards and dashed forward.

"You!" Bale's tone reached a note of maddened hysteria. "You little backstabbing moldwarp! You brought the guards, didn't you?" With a vicious shove, he thrust Olifur forward.

Olifur stumbled and felt himself falling. His stomach hurtled toward his mouth as he began the long descent. His thoughts raced uselessly as he flailed his arms, a scream of terror bubbling in his throat. But before he could act, he felt steady hands catch his arm. He looked into the earnest face of Dojhur: sure-footed, nimble Dojhur, who had darted forward and caught him mid-fall. The older boy's expression tightened with the effort as Olifur swung high above the ground, but a moment later, Garth had joined him and together they pulled Olifur up onto the firm safety of the deck.

"He's getting away," Olifur gasped.

"Get him downstairs," Garth said to Dojhur. "We'll go after the thief."

Dojhur nodded and tucked himself under Olifur's arm, helping him back down the stairs. Outside, the crumpled body of Nneka lying on the ground caught their attention. The two boys ran to her side, kneeling in the dirt.

"Nneka," Olifur whispered brokenly.

She moaned and blinked up at him.

"I tried to get her help," Dojhur whispered. "But she insisted on coming out here after Bale."

Tears glistened in Nneka's eyes. "I tried to stop him from coming tonight. I pleaded and begged. But he was so determined to do wrong. I couldn't see it before, but there's a darkness in his soul. I... I thought I could make him better."

"Only the Builder can make people better," Olifur whispered.

"The Builder," Nneka whispered, and then her eyes closed.

"When I finally found her," Dojhur said, "I wrapped a bandage around her to try and stop the bleeding, but she needs a doctor. Olifur, I'm scared..."

A shout from above made them look up. The guards advanced on Bale's tall, thin silhouette. Their shouts at him to stop trickled down to the ground, where the two boys watched as Bale leaped from one slat to the next in a desperate flight away from his pursuers. The guards shouted orders, and Olifur thought he heard Garth's voice, but the words scattered in the wind. He stared up at the dangerous dance happening above their heads, his heart in his mouth as first one, and then another guard followed Bale carefully out onto the tracks.

Next to him, Nneka whimpered, her breaths coming in sharp, ragged little inhalations. She opened her eyes and stared up at the drama unfolding above them.

Bale's silhouette paused as Garth's voice rang out behind him. The murderer shouted something back.

Then he jumped to the next slat.

With long strides, he leaped again, his long legs propelling him from one slat to the next, away from the Platte and Melar.

"He's getting away," Dojhur muttered angrily.

"STOP!" Garth shouted.

"BALE!" Nneka's voice rose from her throat in agony and despair and burst into the air as though she could not help herself. Olifur stared at her, wondering why. How could she still want to save him after everything?

Olifur never knew if it was because Nneka's voice somehow reached Bale's ears and frightened him all over again, or if it was the powerful, commanding voice of Garth. Perhaps it was a miscalculation in his jump, or just a trick of the slick surface of the train road after all the rain they had gotten, but at that instant, Bale missed his footing. His arms flailed for a moment and his body contorted as he tried to regain his balance. A scream of pure terror filled the night, and then Bale plummeted from the tracks, falling to the ground some seventy feet below.

Olifur felt Nneka shudder as Dojhur turned her face from the scene. In silent agreement, Olifur and Dojhur each put a hand on her shoulders. Together, they knelt beside her while she silently sobbed until Garth and the other guards made it down the stairs and out into the yard. Garth crossed over to them and patted Olifur on the head while shouting for someone to get the doctor. Nneka lay unconscious on the ground, blood seeping out through Dojhur's hastily applied bandages.

Lantern light flared in the windows and Hughin, along with

several other adult overseers, stumbled through the door, blinking blearily around.

"What is going on here?" Hughin barked. His eyes lit on the cart, the crumpled woman lying in the yard, and then they reached Olifur, and his expression wavered between fury and confusion.

Garth stepped forward. "This boy"—he gestured at Olifur—"came to me and told me of a plot to steal from the Platte. He also told me that the thief was the man who had murdered his parents three years ago. With his help, we have brought the criminal to justice."

"Where is this criminal?" Hughin demanded. "Who dared try to rob the Platte? I want him prosecuted to the fullest extent of the law!"

"Sadly, he attempted to flee down the train road," Garth replied. "He missed his jump and fell."

Hughin looked affronted that justice had been so swift, and yet there was little he could do now that the event had already concluded. He sniffed imperiously and muttered about how someone ought to have informed him. Garth replied that it had been his decision to keep as few people involved as possible.

Olifur's attention wandered from the conversation as he turned to Nneka and Dojhur.

The physician approached, along with several orderlies, who carried a stretcher between them. Gently, they lifted Nneka onto it and carried her away. Numbly, Olifur rose to his feet and stumbled after them, uncertain what to do or where to go, but certain that he had no wish to let Nneka out of his sight.

"I will pay for her care." The words came from his heart, but he heard them as though spoken by someone else. It took him a moment to realize that Garth had spoken.

Next to him, Dojhur paced along with him as they followed the doctor and the orderlies away from the Platte and into the street. Nneka's eyes were closed, and Olifur couldn't keep his eyes off the terrible stain of blood that covered the entire front of her dress. Her lips moved, but no sound came from them. Fear gripped him.

"Can you help her?" he asked the physician, who glanced down at him.

The man's eyes were dark and kind. "Let us hope," he replied. "I will do what I can."

Olifur trailed along behind the doctor and the orderlies in the kind of daze that focuses on all the unimportant details: the shapes of the cobblestones, the fluttering moths around the street lanterns, the sting on his neck where Bale's knife had broken the skin, the way his breath caught and burned in the back of his throat, the tears threatening to spill out of his eyes.

"What I just can't understand though"—Olifur heard Hughin's voice rise over the rest of the noise as they left the Platte behind—"is why the thieves were so interested in *empty* cynders."

20

THE BALANCE

Olifur sat next to Nneka's bed, her hand in his. Was it just his imagination, or did her breathing seem more labored today? His mind raced frantically over the past sennight, trying to remember and compare her condition in the times when he could slip away from the Platte to sit by her side.

The door behind him opened, and a small boy, about six years old, poked his head in.

"Oh, hi, Oli," the boy said.

"Hey, Reid," Olifur replied.

"Is Nneka still sleeping?"

"Yeah."

Reid pattered in, a fistful of pink heath clutched tightly between his hands. The little boy looked around for a cup to place them in, and Olifur handed over his own glass of water. Reid dumped the bouquet in and it bobbed sadly and spread out, most of the stems far too short to fill the makeshift vase properly. Reid, however, did not seem to notice, and set this new offering on the already crowded windowsill with the rest. The little boy stood near the bed by Olifur and stared down at Nneka with wide, solemn eyes.

"She'll get better, right, Oli?" he asked in a whisper.

Olifur's heart clenched. "I hope so, Reid."

A little while later, Mikko, Dojhur, and Arim arrived, each with their own flowers or sweet-smelling pastry in hand. They crowded around Nneka's bed, whispering soft words or phrases to her, hoping she might still be able to hear them and know they loved her.

The door opened, and an orderly poked her head inside. When she saw the array of visitors, her lips thinned and she hurried away.

"Good evening, boys." Doctor Sveljen's soft voice made them turn as one to the door. "Might I have a word with you in the hallway?"

They filed out of Nneka's room and into the hall where they stood, fidgeting nervously. But Doctor Sveljen did not look angry. He smiled at them.

"It is good to see that Nneka has such good friends who care about her," he said. "You are all welcome to visit her. But there need to be a few rules. The orderlies need to tend to Nneka, and if there are too many guests at once, they can't do their jobs. Do you understand?"

The boys nodded.

"So two guests at a time. It is good to talk to Nneka, to let her hear your voices, but we also need to give her quiet and rest, so please keep your visits short. And perhaps we could limit the flowers to two bouquets a sennight? Otherwise, I'm afraid the windowsill might give out." The doctor gave them a solemn wink.

Again, the boys nodded.

Now he eyed them sternly. "I know Olifur spends his days working at the Platte. How are the rest of you spending your time?"

There was a general shifting among the boys.

Doctor Sveljen nodded. "That is what I thought. Garth is outside. He came by to pay his respects to Nneka and said that he would be happy to take you boys around and introduce you to some shopkeepers who have been looking for helpers."

The boys filed down the hall to the front doors of the sychstal. As he passed the doctor, Olifur looked up at the tall man.

"Thank you for taking care of her," he murmured.

"Of course," Sveljen replied. "I believe Garth needed to speak with you."

Outside, Olifur greeted the guard who had become his friend. Garth asked him to come down to the guardhouse and answer a few more questions about the night of the robbery. He agreed to do so, grateful for anything that kept him from spending any more time at the Platte than he had to. Hughin had been less than grateful about Olifur's assistance in thwarting Bale's theft. But Garth had fielded the man's suspicions and comments with expert agility and Olifur was grateful to the guard. For his own part, he ignored Hughin as much as possible, kept his head down, did his work well, and collected his stin at the end of each sennight.

After he had given Garth the answers he needed, Olifur headed back to the Platte, his heart heavy. His thoughts traveled to his beloved glen and to Fritjof and his friends. Every extra day he stayed in Melar weighed painfully on his soul. He wondered what was happening back in Elbian. Was Fritjof still alive? He had earned the money needed, but how could he ask Doctor Sveljen to travel so far away from Nneka when she needed his care so desperately? His heart felt as though it were being torn in two. Rubbing a hand over his aching chest, he entered the Platte and made his way to his bed where he fell despondently into a fitful sleep.

———

Days passed. Sennights passed. And still, Nneka slept. Olifur spent as much time as he could at her side, usually staying late into the night after the other boys had their visits. The orderlies were able to feed her broth to keep her alive, but Olifur caught the worried looks they cast at her when they thought he wasn't paying attention.

"Oh, are you still here, young Olifur?"

Olifur, whose head had been nodding toward his chest, jerked to full wakefulness at the good doctor's voice. He turned and grasped at the man's hand.

"Doctor, don't you have any medicine that can heal her?"

Sveljen gazed down at him, his eyes brimming with such kindness Olifur thought he couldn't bear it.

"I am sorry, Olifur," he replied. "Medicine can only do so much." He patted Olifur's head. "Believe it or not, you and the other boys coming in and sitting with her is probably better help than anything more I can provide. Her wound was quite severe, but I am hopeful. What she needs now is rest"—he paused—"and a reason to come back to us." Shaking his head, the doctor sighed. Olifur, sensing that it was near time for his visit to end, rose to leave, but Sveljen placed a gentle hand on his shoulder. "No, you should stay with her tonight. Tomorrow is your rest day, is it not?"

Olifur nodded, amazed at the doctor's ability to remember such a trivial detail.

"Good," Sveljen said. "Then stay. She will need a friendly face if she wakes. I'm not promising anything, mind... but there is a chance."

Olifur sank back down into his chair as the doctor left the room. He picked up Nneka's hand and held it in his own. "Please, Nneka," he whispered. "Please wake up. There's nothing to fear. We will take care of you... all of us... we..." He choked on his tears. "We love you, Nneka. Please..."

He sat and listened to her breathing, her hand clutched in his own. The oil lamp burned on the small table, a tiny bastion of hope surrounded by the darkness of the room. His eyelids grew heavy and his head sank down. He drifted into a doze.

When he woke, he had no idea what time it was. The world outside the window still lay blanketed in darkness. The lamp still gave off a warm glow. Olifur blinked and yawned. Perhaps he should blow out the flame and save the oil. He rolled his shoulders and yawned again, wondering if he should find one of the night-time orderlies and ask for a blanket so he could lie down on the floor.

"Olifur."

He snapped to instant wakefulness as the softest whisper reached his ears. "Nneka?" he breathed, hardly daring to believe. But her fingers tightened around his and her eyes blinked open, squinting as though the lamplight was bright as the midday sun. "Where... am I?"

"You're in the sychstal," Olifur replied. "Do you remember?"

Nneka closed her eyes and his heart sank, but then leaped again as she reopened them. "Water?" she asked, her voice rough.

Olifur sprang to his feet and poured a small cup of water, holding it to her lips for her and gently trickling it into her mouth. Nneka swallowed once and then moaned. He took the cup away and sat down, clutching it in his hands. He wondered if he should call for someone, tell them she had woken, but he couldn't make himself move.

"Bale..." Nneka whispered.

"He's gone, Nneka," Olifur said.

She let out a gentle sigh and gave a single, slow nod. "I'm dying, then."

"Nneka!" Olifur's voice rose in protest, louder than he intended. He saw her flinch at the sound and quickly whispered, "No, Nneka! You can't die. Doctor Sveljen said he hoped you would get well again."

Nneka blinked slowly and shook her head slightly. "I don't... I don't think so."

"I should go get him and let him know you're awake," Olifur said, standing up, his lip jutting out as a stubborn defiance of her words filled him.

Nneka still held his hand, and she tugged at it, halting his progress. "Olifur... please..."

He hesitated, torn between wanting to give her anything she asked for and getting the doctor to come make her better. "Yes, Nneka?"

"I don't..." She winced. "I don't want to die here..."

"You won't!" Olifur protested. "You're going to get well. Doctor Sveljen is the best there is, and he is taking care of you. So you see, you have to get better."

"Please listen, Olifur," Nneka whispered. Her eyes pleaded with him and he relented, sinking back down into his chair. "I don't want to die here in Melar," she rasped. "And if I am to live... I want it to be in your glen. The one you told me of. Please... promise me... don't leave me here..." Her eyes closed and her breathing grew deep and even as unconsciousness claimed her once more.

Olifur bent over her sleeping form. "Anything for you, dear Nneka," he whispered in her ear. Gently, he kissed the back of her hand and then slid it under the blanket before leaving the room to go find Doctor Sveljen. There was much to do and prepare before they returned to the glen. But he would give Nneka this one thing she had asked for; he would not fail her.

———

DOCTOR SVELJEN APPEARED SWIFTLY at Olifur's insistent banging on his door. His eyes were wide, and he had a black case in one hand. "What is it?" he demanded. "Is it Nneka? Is she..."

"She woke up," Olifur interrupted.

"She did?" Doctor Sveljen appeared to relax slightly. "Is she still awake?"

"No," Olifur replied.

"Ah." The doctor nodded. "It happens that way sometimes. That she woke up at all is usually a good sign."

"She wants me to take her to the glen."

"She what?" Sveljen blinked at him.

"She doesn't want to die in Melar," Olifur said, trying not to burst into tears. "She asked me to take her to the glen."

"I see." The doctor fell silent for a moment, his eyes seeming to study something above Olifur's head.

"Doctor?"

"Her injuries were severe," Sveljen said. "And she has been further weakened by sleeping for so long. Moving her so far could kill her."

"She says she's dying already," Olifur mumbled. "If this is to be her last wish... I should... I should try, shouldn't I?" He looked up at the doctor in anguish, wanting the man to tell him what to do, wanting to hear words of comfort.

"Yes," Sveljen said, drawing the word out. He nodded. "Yes," he said more firmly. "I believe in this case the potential benefit outweighs the risk."

Olifur peered up at him, hardly daring to hope. "Doctor, is she dying?"

Sveljen's face filled with compassion. "I do not know," he said. "I have done all I can for her, young Olifur. She is in the Builder's hands, now."

21

HOME

Olifur padded slowly down the road away from Melar. Behind him, Dojhur and the other boys straggled along, ranging themselves behind the cart that Doctor Sveljen was driving. Nneka lay in the cart, bundled in as many blankets and pillows as could be spared in order to keep her still and comfortable on the long journey to the glen. The cart rolled with an aching slowness, for Doctor Sveljen was taking no chances on jostling his patient overmuch.

Olifur walked at the front of the group, unable to rein in his eagerness to get home. And yet it had been harder than he expected to leave Melar, to say his farewells to Garth, Master Epps, and the orderlies at the sychstal who had become his friends during his time hovering over Nneka's bedside.

Master Epps had been the sorriest to see him go.

"Eh, lad," the baker had moaned with exaggerated despair. "Who's going to keep my shop sparkling now? The dust cubs will soon overwhelm me." But he had said it with a sparkle in his eye before wishing Olifur the best of luck and giving him a whole sack of baked goods to take with him.

Garth had given no sign of emotion, but he had shaken Olifur's hand and wished him well with a stern gruffness. Olifur had thanked him again for all his help, but Garth had just given a small shake of his head. "Not at all," he had said.

Now, with his face set homeward, Olifur's spirits lifted within him, feeling lighter than sunshine. He glanced back over his shoulder at his bedraggled little troupe and found a grin spreading across his face. Doctor Sveljen sat on the bench driving the malkyn, his back straight and his eyes alert for any potential bumps. Dojhur and the rest of Bale's crew had begged to return to the glen with Olifur, as well. They wanted a new life somewhere far away from the memories in Melar.

"There are two important rules if you come with me," Olifur had warned them, and they had all agreed to his terms. They were the same terms Fritjof had expected of him when he first came to Fritjof's Glen.

It took them four days before they crested a rise in the road and spotted Elbian ahead. Here, Olifur veered off the main road and led his group down the less-traveled path toward the glen. He did not know if Fritjof still lived, and if he did, he had no idea whether or not he and the other boys were in Elbian or in the glen, but he had to go home. He had to show the glen to Nneka, had to get her there before... He furiously cut his thoughts short, unwilling to contemplate where his mind had been about to travel.

They rumbled slowly down the dusty path. Olifur's heart beat faster. It had been five lunats since he and Bet had headed down the road to Melar. The forest sat in the firm grip of summer. The trees swayed overhead, the emerald canopy protecting them from the sun, fiercely hot even so late in the afternoon. Bursts of color greeted them on every bush, with heath and foxglove nodding along the path and spreading their pinks and purples across the forest floor. As the motley group neared their destination, Olifur was not sure what to expect.

A part of him was certain that Fritjof and the boys had stayed in Elbian, in which case he braced himself for the sight of the glen in disrepair. He half-expected to find his beloved home in shambles, neglected for the winter, and covered in the tattered remains of their absence. However, as they emerged from the trees, he saw immediately that everything was as it should be. A fire smoldered in the enormous hearth. The cabin stood, warm and cozy, and looking bigger somehow. He frowned at it, wondering what was different.

Someone gave a loud shout, and suddenly Kellen was there, pounding him on the back with an enthusiastic greeting and peppering him with questions.

"Where did you go? We looked everywhere for you! Why did you sneak off by yourself like that? Who are all these people? What have you been doing all this time? We thought grymstalkers had eaten you."

Olifur managed a weak grin, but his heart filled with dread. "Fritjof?" The name burst from his lips as his own questions tumbled about in his mind.

Kellen's boisterous bouncing stilled as he noticed the look on his friend's face. "Fritjof lives," he said, easing Olifur's worst fears. "We stayed in Elbian and helped around the village for a few sennights in return for his care. He insisted on returning to the glen come spring." Kellen's expression turned puzzled. "But I thought..."

But just then, Bellamie strode over and lifted him in a bear hug. "You scared us, little Olifur," he reprimanded, interrupting Kellen. "It's good to have you home." He craned his neck and looked behind Olifur. "You've brought guests."

"I brought a doctor from Melar," Olifur said.

Doctor Sveljen reined the malkyn to a halt and stepped down from the cart. "Can I get a hand getting our patient inside the cabin?" he asked.

Kellen and Bellamie led them both to the cabin, Kellen chattering about how they had expanded the cabin to make a more comfortable place for Fritjof to stay.

"It has three whole rooms now!" Kellen announced. "And we're planning on expanding a long room off the back with enough room for all of us before next winter... though we still prefer sleeping outside most of the time."

The doctor carried Nneka inside and the door swung shut in Olifur's face. Feeling useless, he paced about outside for a while. Then he began introducing Kellen to the boys from Melar.

The other boys gathered around now, and Olifur made another round of introductions. Everyone wanted to hear his story, curious about where he had gone, who these newcomers were, and where he had found the doctor. But Olifur found himself suddenly weary beyond reckoning. All the worry and fear and work that he had put into getting to this moment seemed to crash down on him with the suddenness of one of those ocean waves he had glimpsed that night on the beach with Nneka. He sat down against the cabin door and let Dojhur tell most of the story. He let his eyes flutter closed.

They continued to talk as the sun sank down below the trees. Olifur and the other boys from the glen began working on making supper, while telling the boys from Melar to sit and relax.

"The first night, you're guests," Olifur told them, and a warmth spread through him as he remembered Kellen saying the same thing to him. "We'll put you to work tomorrow," he added with a grin.

Supper was eaten, the dishes were washed, new hammocks were strung between trees and low to the ground, and the boys all clambered into them. Olifur swung in his hammock, staring up at the stars with worry and peace warring in his thoughts. The long days of travel eventually caught up with him, however, and he drifted into a troubled sleep.

The next morning, Dojhur and the other boys from Bale's crew, now new initiates in Fritjof's school, were put to work. Olifur showed Reid and Arim how to tend the fire, while Bellamie took Dojhur and Mikko into the woods to gather berries.

About mid-morning, Doctor Sveljen emerged from the cabin and came over to stand by Olifur.

"Nneka is awake," he said. "She handled the journey far better than I expected. In fact, I think the glen is already working a kind of healing on her."

"Will she...?" Olifur couldn't bring himself to finish the question.

"I think with good meals, fresh air, and the kind of care she will receive from you and the other boys here in the glen, there is a good chance that Nneka will recover." Doctor Sveljen smiled. "Would you like to see her?"

Quietly entering the cabin, Olifur's eyes adjusted to the dim light. Across the room, he saw that they had set up a bed near the small fireplace. Nneka lay on the bed, her head propped up on firm pillows. He made his way over to her and sat on the stool next to the bed.

"We're here, Nneka," he whispered. "You're in the glen."

She opened her eyes and gave him a weak smile. "Thank you for bringing me here, Olifur."

"Of course, Nneka. Anything you want..."

"I would like to sit outside and see more of this place."

Olifur hesitated. "I'll ask Doctor Sveljen."

He darted out the door and found Doctor Sveljen, who agreed that sitting outside in the sun would be excellent medicine. Together, they carried Nneka outside and set her on the ground at the base of one of the towering oaks so that she could lean back against its trunk. Nneka gazed around slowly, a bit of color flushing her cheeks as she took in the entirety of Fritjof's Glen.

"Oh, Olifur," she breathed. "It is as beautiful as you said."

Olifur smiled and flopped down beside her. He pointed to the rows of hammocks, and beamed with pride at her astonished look when she saw how high his was hanging from the ground. Then he showed her his bow and recounted the making of it, and how long he had labored over every inch of the stave before it was ready. She handled it with care, running her fingers over the smooth wood, a gentle smile on her lips. As the morning wore on, the other boys returned from their various chores, and Olifur felt he should probably help, but he couldn't quite make himself leave Nneka's side. However, he knew the stew for the midday meal wouldn't cook itself, and so he reluctantly rose.

"Are you all right here, Nneka?" he asked. "Or should you go back to the cabin and get some more rest?"

"I am well for now," she murmured.

"Good," he said.

"Olifur." Nneka's voice arrested him and he turned back to her.

"Yes?"

"Will you..." Nneka's voice came out in a dry rasp. "Will you tell me more about the Builder?"

"I would love to," Olifur replied slowly. "I just wish I could tell the stories as good as Fritjof."

"Well, in that case, perhaps I should tell the stories myself."

The low, gruff voice behind him made Olifur spin around with a glad cry.

"Fritjof!"

And then he had his arms wrapped around the man's waist, and Fritjof was patting his head with a bemused little smile.

"There, there, young Olifur. All is well."

Olifur released his hold on the man and stepped back. Fritjof looked strong and well, his face ruddy with good health and his hair and beard a little mussed as though he had just returned from a hunting trip. Olifur frowned.

"I was so worried..." he began.

Just then, Doctor Sveljen appeared. He strode forward and clasped Fritjof by the hand.

"I see that one of my patients is doing much better," the doctor said.

"Thanks to you," Fritjof replied. "I feel better than I have in years."

"Thanks to Olifur, here." Sveljen nodded his head at the boy.

"Aye," Fritjof returned and tousled Olifur's hair. "Thanks to Olifur."

"But..." Olifur stammered, looking back and forth between the two men. "But how... what... we just got here... how...?"

"Doctor Sveljen has been coming to visit me for many lunats now," Fritjof said, raising an eyebrow. "He said you sent him."

"I... I..." Olifur stared up at Sveljen. "What?"

"I have a confession to make, it seems," Sveljen said, looking a little ashamed. "I had some rounds that took me near Elbian already, so I added a visit to Fritjof a few days after you came to the sychstal and told me your story."

"I was so worried!" Olifur cried. "I was so worried that we would be too late! Why didn't you tell me? I have money. I can pay you!" Olifur paused. "Well, not enough to cover all your visits, but I can earn more. We can all earn more."

"Slow down, Olifur," Doctor Sveljen chuckled. "At first, I stayed silent to protect you. I had no wish to raise false hopes. When I arrived here, Fritjof was very ill, near death. As he responded to my treatments, I grew encouraged but remained uncertain. Then when you and Dojhur brought Nneka to my care, I could not let you bear two such burdens." Sveljen paused and a sudden, pleased grin spread across his face. "As far as payment for his care, Fritjof has bribed me with the finest smoked salmon my wife and I have ever tasted. A couple of more visits to check on my patient will settle that score."

"Thank you," Olifur whispered, and he flung his arms around the doctor, who looked a little startled and then awkwardly patted Olifur on the back.

"Well..." the doctor began and then seemed at a loss for more words. He nodded at Fritjof and held out his hand once more. "I have left instructions with Bellamie for Nneka's care. I will be back in a sennight to check on you both. I am happy to see you looking so well."

The doctor gently extricated himself from Olifur's arms, patted him on the head, and climbed up into the cart. He clucked once to the malkyn, and as the cart rumbled away, Olifur returned his gaze to Fritjof.

"I was so afraid," he mumbled. The weight of all the worry crashed down around him. He had spent so much time terrified that his help would come too late, and now he found himself loath to even blink, almost worried to find that this was all a dream.

"Well, then. The good doctor seems to think I'll be around for a good while longer." Fritjof's face turned thoughtful. "There is a great sadness in that man," he mused. "You can tell he takes joy in serving his fellow man, and in so doing, the Builder himself. But there is a sorrow, as well. The great struggle does not always end so happily." He looked down at Nneka, who sat with her head tilted back, her eyes closed, and a peaceful expression of pure enjoyment on her face. "However, in this story, he will return to find both his patients on the mend, I think."

By this time the other boys had crowded around, introducing the newest members of their little "school" and clamoring to know if Nneka was feeling better.

Fritjof's expression darkened. "That is if those patients can get any peace and quiet around here!" he thundered, but there was a twinkle in his eye and a genuine pride in these, his boys, and their concern for the lady. The general volume decreased, but the boys all seemed to understand instinctively that Fritjof was mostly teasing. He waved the boys away, reminding them that there was work to be done.

Olifur sagged against the tree, relief and happiness coursing through him. He looked up at Fritjof's beloved face, blinking through tears.

The older man smiled down at him. "I am proud of you, lad. It's a remarkable thing you did. I want to hear the whole story."

Olifur nodded wordlessly.

Fritjof glanced down at Nneka. "It appears we have a new project."

Olifur frowned, confused.

"Our lady, Nneka, will need a rocking chair, I think," Fritjof explained. Then he leaned down and lifted Nneka as easily as he would a kitten. "It is time for you to return to bed," he said to her. "This evening, I will tell you of the Builder, but first, you must get some rest." Nneka nodded sleepily and rested her head against Fritjof's shoulder.

Olifur stood at the edge of the glen and savored the scene before him. His friends were working hard while Fritjof gently carried Nneka back to her room, and he could feel his heart swell to bursting. Here were the people he loved best in the world, all gathered together in one place. He thought of all the friends he had made in the past lunats: Garth, and Doctor Sveljen, Master Epps, and more. He wished they could all be here with him. Perhaps that was part of growing up, he thought. Perhaps there would always be small pieces of his heart missing, scattered from town to town, staying with the people he cared about most. But for now, it was enough that these people were here, and that he was home, back in the beauty of his beloved glen.

Olifur leaned against the tree, contemplating all he had lost in his short life, and all he had gained. He tilted his face back and gazed up at the sapphire sky and drank in the familiar scents and smells, the feel of the sunshine on his face and the whisper of the wind through the branches above, green leaves bursting with new life once again.

A rumble sounded behind him and he turned just as Bet's face collided with him in an enthusiastic head-butting nuzzle. He laughed and steadied himself by catching hold of either side of her head, rubbing his own face against her soft nose and breathing in the softness of her fur. She forgave him easily for sending her away, welcoming him back as though he had never left. Then a rustle sounded from the bushes and five tiny malkyn cubs tumbled into the clearing, blinking up at this strange, two-legged friend of their mother's, and Olifur laughed delightedly. He knelt and reached out a hand, fondling the cubs' ears and petting them and exclaiming over them. Looking up, he caught Dojhur's eye and beckoned for him to come over, putting a finger to his lips. Dojhur crept nearer, his eyes wide and his steps soft. Olifur introduced Bet and her brood, and Dojhur's eyes shone with wonder as he made much of the fine litter. Slowly, the other boys made their way over, as well. Soft gasps of admiration and excitement escaped them and they sat on the ground, quietly allowing the cubs to climb over their legs and gnaw on their clothing with tiny, sharp teeth.

Bet butted her head against Olifur again, and he stood. "Are you sure?" he asked.

She gazed at the boys playing with her cubs and gave him a look that said she was confident they'd be looked after. With a grin, Olifur swung himself up onto her back and the malkyn's muscles surged beneath him, carrying them into the forest in great, leaping bounds.

As the wind rushed across his face, fresh and sweet and free, Olifur gave an exultant laugh and thanked the Builder for all he had come through and all he had been given.

It was good.

Don't miss the next installment of ...

A CLASSIC RETOLD

UNEARTH THE TIDES
Alissa J. Zavalianos

Beware the Wasteful Tides
Should the Crimson Death Take You

Huxley Krew Gannon III always knew he would be a royal guard; defending the Crown is in his blood. And coming from a long line of Gannons, that means the job is to be taken seriously at all costs. When tragedy strikes, Huxley is framed for treason, and his only option is to flee to Braka's most-feared place: The Wasteful Tides. It's rumored a monstrous beast haunts those waters, but what Huxley encounters is even worse: an elusive captain, magical herbs, a beautiful lady, and unearthed truths that could change the course of history.

Unearth the Tides is a fantasy retelling of Jules Verne's *20,000 Leagues Under the Sea*. Filled with mystery, found family, and themes of truth and forgiveness, *Unearth the Tides* is perfect for those who love the coziness of the classics and the thrill of adventure.

FROM THE AUTHOR

Thanks for reading!!

These last few pages are ones that I generally assume nobody reads. However, if you are one of the few, the special few, who like to sit in the movies until the credits have all completely finished rolling across the screen, then I salute you as a Kindred Spirit and thank you for being here. I hope you enjoy these last few notes before the final curtain falls.

This story was so much fun to write. It really just came alive for me.

It's a bit strange how much fun it was writing this Oliver Twist retelling. Especially as those who know me will all attest: I've never been the biggest fan of Charles Dickens' writing style. In fact... I really don't like reading him at all!

Don't get me wrong... I love his *stories*, I love his *characters*, I've just never enjoyed his *books!*

So I guess in one sense, it will probably strike most people as very strange that in October 2021, when Allison Tebo first pitched the idea of joining this collaboration of authors retelling classic novels that the first (and only!) story that jumped into my head was one written by none other than Charles Dickens.

But even though I had never read the book, I've always loved the story of Oliver Twist. It's one of my favorite musicals.

Now, I know what you're thinking... surely you didn't write a retelling of a classic novel based solely on seeing a bunch of movie adaptations? I can see your raised eyebrows and your shocked expressions in my mind's eye. "Please, please tell me that you did not do this, Jenelle!"

Let me assure you, that no, I did *not* write this book based solely on the movie adaptations.

I actually read the book.

In fact, the first thing I did, after joining the collaboration, was purchase and read an unabridged copy of Charles Dickens' *Oliver Twist* and read it through for the first time.

And I very greatly disliked it.

But I didn't have a lot of cohesive ideas. I knew what I wanted to do with the characters, but I wasn't sure how to get there. So I asked my dad if he had any ideas, and about an hour later, he sent me a complete book outline.

No joke!

Of course, now I'm not sure if this story really counts as mine. But I am the one who wrote most of the words... so... here you go, Daddy. This book was based on *your* idea.

Honestly, I think the fact that I disliked the original so much was part of what made the writing of this story so very fun... I got to change things! And you, here at the end, having presumably already read the book, unless you're a wonderful weirdo like my dear friend Nicole who flips to the end and reads the credits before reading the story (Yes, I did just put you in a book, Nicole! Lauryn, if you're reading this first, let it be a surprise, ok? I hope this tides you over a bit until Mantles of Oak and Iron comes out... *soon*!) then you already know how much I changed. In fact, you might even argue that the original story was barely there, though I'm hopeful that if you squint really hard you can agree that the outline is still faintly visible through the trees and the magical trains and the giant saber-toothed panthers.

But whether you are an avid Dickens fan and love reading his original works, or you're more like me and you appreciate the stories he wrote but can't handle reading his wordiness and prefer to watch the movie adaptations... I hope that the story you have just finished warmed your heart, entertained you, kept you on the edge of your seat, and made you want more.

If it did any of those things, would you consider leaving me a review on Goodreads? I would be eternally grateful!

If you want more stories like this, you can find all my other books over at my website. If you subscribe to my blog, you'll get a couple of free short stories and you'll be guaranteed to always be informed on what I'm up to and what books are coming out next and when: https://jenelleschmidt.com/subscribe

But before you move on, can I just encourage you to flip back a few pages and read (or re-read) the blurb for the next book in the A Classic Retold series? This group of authors is just so incredibly talented, and all of these stories are truly wonderful. I am honored to be in this series alongside each of them. The year before this collaboration came out, I took the liberty of purchasing books by all of the authors in the collaboration whom I hadn't read before, and every single one of them made it into my Top Favorite Fantasy Reads for the year. I am so proud to be published along-side each and every one of these authors, and I highly and whole-heartedly and unreservedly recommend their books in this series and the other books they have published, as well.

Happy reading!

ABOUT THE AUTHOR

Jenelle first fell in love with stories through her father's voice reading books aloud each night. A relentless opener-of-doors in hopes of someday finding a passage to Narnia, it was only natural that she soon began making up fantastical realms of her own. Jenelle currently resides in the wintry tundra of Wisconsin — which she maintains is almost as good as Narnia — with her knight-in-shining armor and their four hobbits. When she is not writing, she homeschools said hobbits and helps them along on their daily adventures... which she says makes her a wizard.

9 781960 357984